A
Harlequin
Romance

OTHER
Harlequin Romances
by LUCY GILLEN

Many of these titles are available at your local bookseller,
or through the Harlequin Reader Service.

For a free catalogue listing all available Harlequin Romances,
send your name and address to:

HARLEQUIN READER SERVICE,
M.P.O. Box 707, Niagara Falls, N.Y. 14302
Canadian address: Stratford, Ontario, Canada.

or use order coupon at back of book.

THE
CHANGING YEARS

by

LUCY GILLEN

HARLEQUIN BOOKS   TORONTO
WINNIPEG

Original hard cover edition published in 1972
by Mills & Boon Limited.

© Lucy Gillen 1972

SBN 373-01847-9

Harlequin edition published January 1975

1847

CHAPTER ONE

NOTHING had changed, April noted with relief. The house
still sat, square and safe, amid its protective huddle of
trees, windows beaming almost smugly in the hot July
sun. As the taxi brought her along the short, tree-shaded
driveway she remembered the last time she had been at
Kinley, almost seven years ago.

Uncle Simon had always been something of a mystery
to her, as he was to the rest of his family, and his eccen-
tricity had puzzled, and at times frightened, her a little,
for a fifteen-year-old girl can be very impressionable.

Being an orphan she had been in charge of her Aunt
Betty at the time, and Aunt Betty had taken swift and
unhesitating advantage of the unexpected invitation to
stay at Kinley. Simon Carver was, in fact, April's great-
uncle and Aunt Betty and he were niece and uncle and
not usually on the best of terms.

When she was old enough to reason it for herself April
suspected that financial differences were the main cause of
the dissension between them, for Uncle Simon was
wealthy beyond anything April could imagine, while
Aunt Betty managed on a small but adequate income left
to her by her husband.

They had stayed at Kinley for four whole months and
then, almost inevitably, he and his niece had quarrelled
and April found one morning that she was required to
pack her bags and leave in company with an indignant
and tearful Aunt Betty. She remembered standing in the
hallway with her suitcases beside her, waiting for a taxi to
come and take them to the station, with Aunt Betty red-
eyed and stiffly silent, and Nick risking his stepfather's

wrath to bid them goodbye.

Nick Lawton had been the brightest spot in the whole of that four months' stay, and the older version of April that was now on her way back to Kinley recognized her earlier feelings for him with a wry smile. It had been purely and simply schoolgirl idolatry, and she must have been a great trial to him, for he was already a grown man and probably embarrassed by her painful and very obvious crush on him.

He had given no sign that he was uneasy about it, however, but had treated her with a gentle kindness, especially when she shrank from Uncle Simon's brusque and often unkind tongue. Nick had even taught her to ride, although she had proved a not very apt pupil and never became really proficient.

Ten years older than April, he had seemed incredibly tall and attractive, and she could not think that he would have changed so much in seven years, certainly not as much as she had herself. She looked forward to seeing Nick again.

Uncle Simon had married very late in life and had acquired a young stepson at the same time as his much younger wife. He had never quite recovered from her death at a comparatively early age and he became even more of a recluse, and yet more eccentric, although his stepson seemed to find him acceptable company and stayed on with the old man.

Uncle Simon had issued the present invitation out of the blue, as he had done before, only this time Aunt Betty had been excluded, and April could not help being sorry about that. Not that April lived with her aunt still, for she had moved to London three years before, determined to be more independent and to try out her wings, working as a commercial artist with an advertising firm.

Uncle Simon's letter had been brief and, inevitably,

6

vague, but she had gathered the drift of it easily enough and thought long and deeply about her decision. He had requested, in terms that showed he had no thoughts of being refused, that she leave her job and come and stay at Kinley for a month or two. It would, he intimated, be worth her while, for he had very little longer to live and he was not a poor man by any means.

Initially, the bluntness of the letter had shocked her, but then she realized that it was merely typical of Uncle Simon and he was, after all, eighty-two years old. Giving up her job was rather a rash thing to do, perhaps, but April was inclined to be impulsive and curiosity was rearing its head; also she was undeniably curious to see Nick again.

She had had a number of boy-friends since her move to London and independence, but she had never found anyone that she considered sufficiently interesting to take seriously, and now, when she considered it, she wondered if her early attraction to Nick had in some way influenced her without her realizing it.

She smiled when she considered the idea and was unaware of the taxi-driver's quick, interested look in the mirror as she did so. Shorter than average, she was what is generally recognized as petite, and in the short, sleeveless dress she wore looked scarcely older than she had seven years before.

Short brown hair framed a face that was more than merely pretty, with a small, retroussé nose and huge, dark-fringed blue eyes. The mouth that smiled so reminiscently was perhaps a trifle too wide for conventional beauty, but it was soft and pretty and looked as if it smiled a lot.

'Here we are, miss.' The taxi-driver lifted her cases out for her and deposited them on the drive, touching his cap briefly before he drove off.

April looked around her hopefully, but no one appeared at the front door, so probably her arrival had gone unnoticed. She tried picking up the two big suitcases, but found them much too heavy for her and immediately put them down again. Surely someone must be about to welcome her; they knew what time she was arriving. She was about to ring, rather hesitantly, on the front door bell when she heard a car coming along the drive and turned swiftly.

The rather opulent-looking vehicle braked to a halt almost beside her and she realized with a start that the driver was Nick Lawton. There was no mistaking that brown, lean face and she was quite startled to see him looking so little older than she remembered him. But of course there would be a much less noticeable difference in an already grown man than in the schoolgirl she had been the last time she was here.

He got out of the car, already smiling, and extended a hand in welcome, while April fought to subdue an embarrassing return of the schoolgirl crush she had thought outgrown. He still seemed incredibly tall, something over six feet, she guessed, and the brown eyes, with that ever so slight upward tilt at their outer corners, looked down at her speculatively, long fingers impatiently brushing back a fall of dark hair from his forehead.

'April?' She nodded as strong fingers closed round her hand and held it so for several seconds while he studied her. 'Very nice,' he said at last. 'You've definitely improved with age.'

It was not the greeting she had expected and she felt he was laughing at her, though she could not imagine why. 'Hello, Nick.' She wished she could do something about the erratic thudding of her heart when he held her hand. It was quite ridiculous to behave like a schoolgirl still when she was a grown woman. 'You haven't changed,' she said, and wondered as she spoke if he had perhaps changed more than she realized.

His gaze left her face and swept slowly over her from top to toe and back again and he smiled. '*You* have,' he told her.

'I'm older, and on me it shows more.' She tried to keep her voice steady and to sound light and casual about it, but something of the old magic still remained.

'Women and wine improve with age, they say,' he quoted, and smiled again, as if something was still amusing him. He glanced down at her cases. 'I missed you at the station,' he told her. 'I suppose you went out of the back way, didn't you? Without looking to see if anyone was waiting for you.'

April shook her head. 'I may have done,' she admitted. 'I just went through the nearest door. I didn't realize anyone would be meeting me.'

'You should have,' he informed her. 'I suppose you were dumped here like orphan Annie and left to fend for yourself, and that, if I remember rightly, was something you're not very good at.'

He picked up the two heavy cases with little apparent effort and April followed him, frowning over his opinion of her helplessness. 'I'm perfectly capable of fending for myself,' she said. 'I've been living in London on my own for three years now and I manage very well.'

He heaved a shoulder on the solid-looking door, and it creaked open, grinning at her as he did so. The hinges creaked alarmingly and April was reminded of her last visit. It seemed incredible that such a small thing could still remain in her memory, but she remembered those hinges creaking like that before and she smiled as she commented on it.

'You still haven't oiled those hinges, I see,' she said, and saw one dark brow express surprise.

9

'What a memory you have for trivia,' he remarked. 'Were they creaking when you were here before?'

'Just like that,' April said. 'I remember it quite vividly.'

'If it's that long,' he said, 'I must get Widgeon on to it.'

'Widgeon?'

He nodded. '*Some* things have changed while you've been away,' he told her. 'We now have a quite profitable breeding stable, and Widgeon helps out, both there and in the house, doing odd jobs.'

'Oh, I see.' The news surprised her, although it should not have been too much of a surprise to know that Nick was working with horses, for he had always loved them and rode whenever he had the opportunity. 'I suppose you haven't still got old Cobber, have you?'

He dumped her cases down and pulled a wry face as he shook his head. 'Poor old Cobber's gone, but his progeny are going strong – the old boy started a good line.' He looked at her quizzically, his eyes crinkled at their corners in a smile. 'Are you still a lousy rider?' he asked.

April pouted reproach, thinking that the old Nick would never have been so outspokenly unkind to her. 'I haven't ridden since I was here last,' she told him. 'I don't suppose I could even remember how to start now.'

He nodded. 'I'll soon get you in trim again,' he informed her confidently. 'It'll be good for you after all that high living in the big city.' A long finger reached out and touched her cheek in a gesture that was both caress and invitation to comment. 'You've got a pavement tan, although I'm not averse to the pink and white image for a change.'

April turned her face away from his touch and felt the colour in her cheeks as she looked around her at the big, cool hall, determined to change the subject to something far less personal, although she realized that seven years ago she would have given her right arm to have had Nick behave as he was now.

The hall looked almost exactly as it had last time she saw it, but there was a subtle difference that was most noticeable in the nearly new rugs on the tiled floor and the way the dark wood glowed with polishing and the brass gleamed in the light.

Seeing her interest in her surroundings, Nick Lawton smiled. 'I talked Pop into taking on a full-time house-keeper,' he informed her. 'It looks a bit less neglected, doesn't it?'

She had to agree that it did and nodded agreement. 'It looks beautiful,' she said, and turned sharply when a door behind them opened and a woman came out into the hall. The door from the kitchen, April remembered.

Nick smiled at the newcomer, a short, stout, elderly woman, and indicated April's two suitcases. 'Our visitor's arrived,' he said. 'April, this is Mrs. Widgeon, the source of all this spit and polish.' He gave the two of them barely time to acknowledge the introduction before he picked up the luggage and started up the stairs with it, April following, a little uncertainly.

The room on the right, immediately at the top of the stairs, had been hers before and she rather hoped it would again, for it had a superb view from its windows. Nick put down one of the cases and opened the door, looking at her over one shoulder as he did so. 'You're in the same room as before,' he told her.

'I remember.'

He dumped her cases down at the end of the same brassily ornate iron bed, and grinned. 'I'll bet you don't,' he said. 'It's been redecorated in your honour.'

It had indeed been redecorated and April smiled her pleasure at the change. Last time it had been so dark –

dark painted woodwork and dark red papered walls; now it had sunshine yellow walls and the paintwork was glistening white. 'It's lovely,' she declared, crossing to the big bed and bouncing it experimentally. 'And so bright.'

'Better than dark red and brown?' he asked, obviously pleased with her reaction so that she wondered how much he had influenced the change.

April nodded. 'Much better,' she agreed. Turning to face him, she felt more shy than she had ever done in her gauche, schoolgirl days. He stood in the middle of the room studying her. Those slightly tip-tilted eyes had seemed dreamily attractive to her fifteen-year-old image, now they looked strange and somehow oddly menacing as they watched her from the lean, brown face half shadowed as he stood with his back to the window. 'Did you choose the colour scheme, Nick?'

'Of course; I knew you'd like it.' She did not remember thinking him arrogant before, now the word came unbidden to her mind and she began to see him in a new light. Physically he might have looked exactly the same, but either he had changed in some subtle way or she was now aware of things she had not noticed before.

There was a definite glint of amusement behind the expression in his eyes, and he had an easy self-confidence that gave the impression he would be at ease wherever he was. She had experienced too many looks of admiring speculation not to recognize what lay behind the slow sweeping gaze he covered her with, until it came to rest on her mouth and he smiled.

'I'd have chosen something a bit more exotic if I'd realized what a beauty you'd grown into,' he told her softly.

She remembered his voice as deep and soft, but she had never recognized it for the seductive weapon it undoubtedly was until now, and she felt the swift warm colour in her cheeks again as she turned her back on him, smoothing a hand over the yellow silk coverlet that felt cool and soft under her fingers. 'I don't like over-exotic rooms,' she said. 'I like this one just as it is.' He said nothing and she turned back, sensing that he expected something of her in the way of curiosity. 'Nick, why did Uncle Simon ask me to come and stay here?'

He smiled, holding her gaze. 'Why did you come?' he countered.

'I don't know.' She moved away from the bed and over to the window. 'Curiosity, I suppose,' she admitted, and he laughed softly, so that she looked over a shoulder at him.

'Not because you're mercenary?' he asked, and April flushed.

'What do you mean?'

He was still smiling, one hand in a pocket, completely at ease and quite uncaring whether she took offence at what he said or not. 'I read the letter Pop sent you, April. It hinted at things that would make any woman's mercenary streak show itself – and here you are!'

'You mean—' She stared at him for a moment, horrified to think that he had such a low opinion of her, but very uncertain how right he was. 'You have no right to suggest that I came here simply because – because Uncle Simon's – well, better off than most,' she told him.

'What other reason could there be?' he asked, blandly unconcerned that he had offended her.

She hesitated, her eyes wary, looking at him from under her lashes. 'He *is* my uncle,' she said at last.

'And you haven't seen him for seven years.'

'That wasn't my fault,' April objected. 'He quarrelled with Aunt Betty and I was living with Aunt Betty at the time, I couldn't very well defy her. Anyway,' she added, 'he didn't like me.'

Nick shook his head. 'Of course he did,' he argued. 'You didn't undertand him very well, April.'

'But he was always so – so rough and brusque,' April insisted.

'It's his way, and it's not just reserved for you either. He never speaks or acts any differently.'

'Still?' She looked less than enthusiastic at the idea of meeting her great-uncle again, especially when Nick nodded his head with a faint grin, recognizing her fears.

'He won't eat you,' he promised.

'He used to frighten the life out of me before,' April confessed ruefully. 'That's why I was so grateful to you.'

He looked surprised as if he could not follow her reasoning. 'Grateful?' he asked, one brow arched quizzically. 'I can't imagine what for.'

'You were very kind to me, Nick, and I—' She stopped herself in time from confessing to that embarrassing schoolgirl crush.

'You had the most almighty crush on me,' he finished for her, and laughed deeply at her frown of embarrassment.

'I'm glad you found it amusing,' she said shortly. 'I'd have curled up and died if I'd realized you knew.'

'I couldn't very well *not* know,' he laughed, obviously relishing the memory. 'You used to follow me around, goo-eyed, everywhere I went.'

Seeing her teenage dream so rudely shattered, April frowned, deciding that Nick Lawton had definitely not improved with age. 'I'm sorry if I embarrassed you,' she told him. 'But at least you won't have that to contend with while I'm here this time.'

His sigh was exaggerated and, she felt sure, completely

insincere. 'This time I wouldn't object in the least,' he informed her.

It was something of a shock meeting Uncle Simon again, and April wished Nick had warned her how much the old man had changed. Seven years ago he had been an elderly man, now he was an old one. He was a year or so beyond eighty, of course, but the narrow blue eyes that looked at her from under bushy grey brows had a sharp, alert look that seemed not to have diminished with the years. In fact as she saw him first she felt like a small girl again and almost hid her head.

'April?' A long thin hand waved her forward impatiently.

'Hello, Uncle Simon.'

She was uncertain whether or not she was expected to kiss him, but she hesitated to take the liberty until she was more certain. 'Well, come here, girl, come here.' The voice was as thin and waspish as ever, but imperious, as if he was accustomed to having his every wish obeyed promptly, and he beckoned her closer still. His eyes narrowed as he peered at her and she realized that despite their apparent sharpness, they were very weak. She came and stood close to his chair, a sudden and quite unexpected feeling of pity catching at her throat.

'It's nice to see you again, Uncle Simon.'

He ignored the nicety and instead stared at her almost rudely. 'You're a pretty enough gel, now you're out of the gawky stage,' he declared, and April had the sudden desire to giggle, for it was surely the most ungracious compliment she had ever received.

'Thank you,' she said solemnly.

'How old are you now?' The question was abrupt and she wondered at his interest in such trivia.

'I'm twenty-two, Uncle Simon.'

15

'You're not married?'

'I'm not married,' she agreed, preparing to be interrogated.

'Hmm.' The grey head nodded, as if the answer pleased him. 'You know I'm a very wealthy man, my girl?'

The question was unexpected and she nodded slowly, reminded of Nick Lawton's opinion that she had accepted the old man's invitation for purely mercenary reasons, and hoping her great-uncle was not of the same opinion. 'Yes,' she admitted. 'Yes, I do know, Uncle Simon.'

The narrow blue eyes squinted up at her. 'That why you came?'

April looked at him indignantly, wishing she had never been so foolish as to accept that blunt but intriguing invitation. 'I've already been accused of having mercenary motives,' she told him, 'and I don't like the implication, Uncle Simon. If that's what you think of me why did you ask me to come here?'

He was silent for a moment, then surprisingly, he chuckled. 'You've got spirit,' he approved. 'I like that in a woman.' The narrow eyes studied her speculatively. 'So young Nick stepped on your toes too, did he?' he asked, and April smiled wryly.

'If you can call it that,' she allowed. 'He seemed to think I was here simply because you were a very wealthy relation, and it's not true. I *was* curious,' she added, truthfully, 'and I suppose I had the fact that you're a very rich man at the back of my mind, but it wasn't my prime motive, whether you and Nick believe it or not.'

'I wanted you here because I haven't got much longer,' the old man told her bluntly. 'I haven't seen you for seven years and I didn't know if you'd grow up to be like that damned stupid aunt of yours – had to make sure first.'

'First?' April looked intrigued.

'Before I made my will again,' he told her. 'Couldn't go

leaving half my money to some silly chit who wouldn't know how to handle it. You might have grown to be as big a fool as your aunt.'

'Aunt Betty was very good to me,' April told him firmly, refusing to hear any ill of her aunt. 'And I'd have been quite happy to grow up like her, Uncle Simon.'

'Huh! Much good may it have done you.' The narrow eyes gleamed maliciously. 'You and Nick are the only two in my family I care two hoots for and you two'll get my money – now I've seen you.'

'I'm – I'm very grateful, Uncle Simon.'

'Grateful?'

'That you're being so generous. I expected you to leave everything you have to Nick. After all, he's your stepson and he's been with you most of his life.'

'He'll do all right,' the old man declared. He looked at her steadily for a moment. 'Did you say you'd been arguing with Nick?' he asked, and April shook her head in denial.

'Not arguing, Uncle Simon, we haven't seen enough of each other for that.' She almost added 'yet' but thought better of it. 'Nick's changed,' she said thoughtfully, and the old man shook his head.

'Nick's the same as he always was,' he declared. 'It's you who've changed, my girl. You used to follow him around like an adoring pup.'

'We've been through all that, Uncle Simon,' she said. 'It seems I was the cause of a good deal of amusement.'

'Is that what he told you?'

April nodded. 'I believe him too. I can imagine that being adored so persistently by a fifteen-year-old must have been highly amusing, when it wasn't annoying.'

'You were a pretty child for all your gawkiness,' he told her, 'and Nick was no more averse to being hero-worshipped than anyone else.'

'I don't suppose he was,' April agreed, 'but I've told him he doesn't have to worry about that this time.'

'You're over your hero-worship?'

'Of course, I'm not a schoolgirl now.'

'You've got no young man courting you?'

The conversation, April felt, was becoming unreasonably personal, but she tried not to take offence. 'I've several boy-friends, Uncle Simon,' she told him, 'but none very serious.'

'It's as well,' the old man declared firmly. 'Schoolgirl silliness is all very well, but I wouldn't have been very impressed if you were prepared to marry the first young idiot who asked you.'

April was awake early the following morning and it took her a moment or two to realize where she was. When she did she lay wondering what on earth had possessed her great-uncle to invite her to Kinley simply so that he could inspect her and see if she was worth leaving anything in his will. It was typical of him that he had not considered having her over for just a day, but had specified that the visit should extend two or three months.

However – she shrugged, watching a long finger of sunlight poking between the curtains and pointing across her bed to the opposite wall – there was no harm in enjoying her stay for as long as it lasted, especially if it resulted in her becoming a rich woman one day. She hastily dismissed such mercenary thoughts and blinked at the disturbing sunlight. Better get up and go in search of the breakfast she could smell from the kitchen below her room.

She found she was to have only the company of Nick for breakfast and once again experienced that annoying sense of shyness when she saw him there in the big, white-walled room she remembered so well.

He rose when she came in, then sat himself down again and got on with his already half-eaten breakfast. 'You're bright and early,' he remarked, looking at her across the table, while she tried not to notice the way a snowy white tee-shirt showed off the strong brown throat and arms and the dark face with its intriguing eyes.

'I'm used to being up fairly early,' she told him, and carefully poured herself coffee from the enormous pot he put within her reach.

'Would you care to come down to the stable with me?'

She looked at him curiously for a second, then remembered that he was now the proud owner of a small stud. She nodded. 'Yes, thank you, Nick, I'd like to see your horses.'

'We've some foals you can coo over,' he told her with a gleam in his eye that invited her to object to his choice of words.

'Oh, lovely!' She refused to be baited so early in the morning, and told herself she would try hard not to be touchy about his obvious intention to tease her at every opportunity. 'How many?'

'Two. They arrived within a couple of hours of each other a week ago. It was quite a night.'

'I can imagine.' She drank her coffee and buttered some toast, wondering if he was prepared to wait for her to have breakfast, and got her answer sooner than she expected.

He got up from the table with a murmur of excuse and smiled broadly at her. 'You can find your own way down to the stables, can't you?' he asked, and she nodded.

'Yes, I think I remember where they are.'

'O.K. I'll see you when you've had breakfast.' He was gone with a careless wave of one hand and April was left looking after him curiously.

It was obvious that he was very proud of his new venture and she wondered if it was his independent spirit that had made him do something to earn his own living rather than live a comfortable life of ease at his step-father's expense, as he could quite easily have done.

She finished her breakfast and Mrs. Widgeon saw her off to the stable with a friendly smile. There was quite a lot of land belonging to Kinley and the gardens at the back of the house were enchanting at this time of year. There were roses in profusion which Nick's mother had planted, so Nick had told her once, and a smooth green lawn that looked much more inviting than the rough yard that led to the stables.

She found Nick without too much trouble and duly admired the new arrivals, delighted with the long-legged grace of the two little creatures as they skipped and played round the paddock. It was when they went back to the field at the other end of the yard that April began to have doubts about the wisdom of coming out here.

There were two animals grazing quietly on the short grass, a tall bay and a shorter-legged roan who reminded her of Cobber, the horse she had learned to ride on. Nick glanced at her as they leaned on the fence, his unusual eyes glittering with what she recognized as a challenge.

'That's Cobber's grandson,' he informed her, pointing to the roan. 'Do you think you could ride him?'

April looked at the strong-looking animal warily, and then at Nick. 'I'm sure I couldn't,' she told him. 'It's seven years since I was on a horse of any sort and he looks as if he might be frisky.'

'Oh, nonsense,' Nick jeered, calling the roan over to the fence. 'He's as quiet as a lamb, aren't you, old boy?'

'I'd sooner take your word for it,' April insisted. 'I'm not cut out for horse-riding, Nick.'

He laughed, his eyes crinkling at their corners, a hint of

mockery in the sound of it for her nervousness. 'You're cut out for anything that shows off that dishy figure of yours,' he told her. 'You're just a natural born coward, April Summers.'

'I'm *not* a coward,' April denied indignantly. 'I'm just not a horsey type, that's all.'

'That I agree with,' he said, 'but that doesn't mean you can't ride. Come on, April, be a sporting trier at least.'

'No!' She would have moved away, but the roan's soft nose pushed itself into her clenched hands on top of the fence and she instinctively responded to the invitation to fuss. 'He's lovely,' she said more quietly, 'and just like dear old Cobber.'

'Then why not trust him?' Nick suggested.

'No, Nick, I'm not making a fool of myself just to provide you with something to laugh at. You had your share of that when I was here before.'

'Oh, I didn't laugh at you,' he denied, his eyes glittering wickedly in a way that gave lie to his words. 'Honest I didn't.'

'You admitted you did,' she reminded him. 'And I could curl up every time I think of the way I used to gaze at you so adoringly, grateful for every smile you gave me and every word.'

He was laughing openly now, and she could feel the colour warm in her cheeks, turning away from him when she could no longer bear to face his obvious amusement. 'Oh, you were such a sweet little slave,' he said. 'I wasn't really too cruel to you, was I, April? I tried not to be.'

'I – I suppose not,' she admitted. 'I thought you were very kind to me at the time, it's only now that I can see what an utter and complete fool I was.'

'You were very young.' He spoke softly and she recognized the effectiveness of that deep soft voice again as she looked at him briefly before lowering her eyes. One hand

21

reached out and touched her cheek and for a moment she was her fifteen-year-old self again, resting her face against his hand for a second before she realized what she was doing, and drew back.

'I have that excuse,' she admitted, 'but it would have been much better not to have seen you again, Nick, after so long.'

'Have your illusions been shattered?' He was smiling at her in a way she would have given her right arm to see before.

'Yes,' she told him bluntly, determined to shatter them once and for all. 'I suppose it's always a mistake to go back, isn't it?'

'Sometimes.' He put his other hand to her face and held her there for a long moment before he bent and kissed her mouth slowly and with infinite gentleness so that she closed her eyes and leaned her head back against the strong fingers that held her.

'Nick!' She opened her eyes and looked up at him aghast to find her heart hammering away wildly at her ribs and the colour warm in her cheeks. She moved her head and broke his hold, laughing a little breathlessly as she smoothed back her hair with both hands. 'Seven years ago,' she told him, 'I'd have swooned clear away if you'd done that. It's a good job I've grown up.'

'It's a *very* good job you've grown up,' he echoed softly, and laughed. 'It's more fun now.'

CHAPTER TWO

APRIL was very tempted the following morning to have her breakfast later, when she expected Nick would have finished his and gone, but she thought if she did he might possibly read some significance into it following yesterday's episode.

He looked up and grinned when she came in, getting up briefly until she was seated. 'You look fresh and beautiful,' he told her. 'Do you always look so good first thing in the morning?'

'I – I try.' She wished she could control the runaway pulse that always responded to his voice.

'You succeed,' he assured her. 'You'll brighten some lucky husband's working life one day.'

She took up the huge coffee pot and poured herself a steadying drink, deciding not to rise to the so obvious bait. 'It's much too nice to stay in,' she said. 'I like to make the most of this lovely weather.'

'What are you doing today?'

She looked up at him curiously, suspecting something other than simple curiosity behind the question. 'I don't know,' she said. 'I hadn't really thought about it.'

'Good!' She blinked enquiringly, and he grinned. 'We can go riding.'

'Riding?' April frowned. He knew how she felt about attempting to ride again and she determined not to let him talk her round.

'You know – on horses.'

'I know,' she said. 'But you know I don't like the idea, Nick, I was never any good at it and I've no great desire to try again.'

'Oh, you'll be O.K. with me.'

He was already taking it for granted that she would comply as she would once have done willingly. His arrogant self-assurance was something she was rapidly beginning to recognize as part of his character and she was blessed if she was going to be browbeaten by it.

'I'm not so sure,' she told him shortly. 'Anyway, I don't want to go, and that's a good enough reason. You know, it's useless trying to make a horsewoman out of me, Nick.'

The inevitable laughter was already showing itself. 'You could at least try,' he said, and looked at her from under half-closed lids. 'You had much more spunk when you were a kid,' he added by way of a goad.

April flushed. 'I was prepared to do almost anything to please you then,' she admitted. 'Regardless of how big a fool I made of myself.'

'But what can you lose?' He spread his hands, his eyes fixed on her relentlessly, determined to get his own way, as she was just as determined not to let him. 'You can't have forgotten everything I taught you,' he said.

'No, Nick, I can't do it.'

'Of course you can,' he insisted, and leaned across the table to cover one of her hands with his. 'Just to please me.' April was horrified to feel her heart hammering away crazily at her ribs and she hastily withdrew her hand, refusing to meet the gaze she knew was seeking to weaken her resolve. 'You'd have done it once,' he added softly. 'Just to please me.'

She shook her head, hating to be reminded yet again of her youthful folly. 'I know I would,' she admitted, 'but it's different now, Nick, and I—'

'You don't care whether you please me or not, eh?' The brown eyes held a hint of laughter as well as impatience when she at last looked up at him. 'Also,' he added softly, 'you're scared.'

'I am scared,' she agreed shortly, 'and nothing you say will persuade me ever to get on a horse again.'

'Never?'

'Never,' she insisted.

They were both silent for a while, the air between them heavy with unspoken questions and words best left unsaid, then Nick looked up, caught her eye and laughed. 'Stalemate,' he said. 'Well, at least I tried. I'm going over to Jordan's this morning and I rather wanted you to come with me, but if I can't persuade you—' He shrugged and April frowned, the name Jordan's striking a familiar chord in her memory.

'Jordan's?'

He smiled, pleased to have caught her attention. 'You remember it?'

'Yes. At least I think I do.' She frowned uncertainly. 'Wasn't there a – a Dick Jordan, or something like that?'

Nick laughed, nodding agreement. 'There was, only his name's Donald, and he remembers you rather better than you do him, obviously.'

'Does he?' She looked a little startled at the information, but the memory was becoming more clear now. A tall, thin, fair-haired boy, a couple of years older than herself, who had gazed at her in much the same way as she had looked at Nick, only she had not realized the significance of it at the time. 'I – I think I remember him,' she said.

'Poor old Donald,' Nick declared feelingly. 'He'd be very hurt if he thought you'd forgotten him.'

'It's a long time ago,' April told him. 'I can't be expected to remember everyone I met.'

'And such a devoted admirer too.' The brown eyes taunted her. 'It's a good job *I* haven't got such a short memory for *your* youthful passions.'

'I wish to heaven you had,' April was stung to retort. 'I'm sick of being reminded of how stupid I was seven years ago!'

He rested one elbow on the table and propped his chin on the hand, looking at her down his nose, undisguisedly amused. 'Isn't there just a faint hint of adoration left?' he asked, and April bit her lip, shaking her head in vehement denial.

'Not a hint,' she denied, and met his eyes defiantly. 'I've outgrown you, Nick, I'm not a little girl any more.'

He sighed, deeply and apparently sincerely, and looked at her with a kind of sadness she could almost believe. 'It's a pity,' he told her. 'Being adored by a girl like you would have been very good for my ego.'

'Your ego,' April informed him shortly, 'doesn't need any encouragment, it's thriving without my help.'

For a moment he said nothing, but his eyes gleamed with something she could not quite interpret. 'What is it the old adage says?' he suggested softly. 'Hell hath no fury—' He laughed when she glared at him furiously. 'I wonder what Donald Jordan's going to think of you now.'

'I'm not going with you,' April said firmly. 'So you're not likely to find out.'

'I was thinking,' he said slowly, after a moment's thoughtful silence. 'It might be a good idea if you made yourself useful while you're here.' She eyed him suspiciously. 'If you were to exercise Dingo for me, it would be very useful. Dingo's the roan,' he added by way of explanation.

'I don't quite see—' April began. 'Do you think I *should* make myself – useful?'

He shrugged again, a faint smile touching his mouth.

'If you want to impress Pop,' he told her, 'you could do worse than turn your hand to helping me. He admires industry.'

'I'm not trying to impress Uncle Simon,' she denied. 'Not for the reason you mean, anyway, but if you think he expects me to – to earn my keep then I'm quite willing to do anything within reason.'

'Mrs. Widgeon won't take kindly to you helping in the house,' he told her, 'so that leaves the stables.' She looked at him in dismay, having visions of all manner of filthy jobs coming her way. 'Just exercising the horses,' he assured her with a grin. 'It's not a very arduous chore.'

She was silent for a moment, seeing herself trapped into the very situation she had been determined to avoid, and not at all sure that it wasn't just a trick of his. Uncle Simon was certainly a fiercely independent man, despite his wealth, and he had little patience with those who did nothing for their living, so it was just possible that he would expect her to make herself useful while she was there.

'All right,' she sighed at last. 'I'll ride your blessed horse for you. But not dressed like this.'

He swept a swift expressive glance over her short, sleeveless dress and smiled. 'No. Beautiful as you look in that brief piece of enchantment, trousers would be more practical.'

He was waiting in the hall for her when she came downstairs some time later dressed in a pair of white denim trousers and a pale blue shirt, and he nodded his approval. She looked incredibly slim and shapely as well as practical and somehow managed to appear even tinier.

'You look delicious,' he informed her. 'The belle of the ball.'

'Except that I'm expected to act as groom instead of

Cinderella,' April retorted, but flushed pink nevertheless.

'You better go in and tell Pop what you're doing,' he
told her. 'He'd like to know.'

The old man looked at her narrowly when she walked
into the room, followed by Nick. 'I've been roped in to ride
one of Nick's horses,' she told him without preamble. 'At
least I'm going to try.'

'Good, good.' He seemed to approve, as Nick had said
he would. 'I like to see a girl making herself useful. Too
many of 'em sit and do nothing these days.'

'I'll probably make a complete fool of myself,' April
said, as the old man beckoned her over, his head nodding
approval as she came closer.

'You're a good-looking girl,' he told her, ignoring the
complaint, and April smiled resignedly. She was beginning
to recognize the truth of Nick's assertion that the old
man's bark was much worse than his bite.

'Thank you, Uncle Simon.'

'You're sure you haven't got some young buck waiting
to marry you, back in London?'

April shook her head. 'No one serious, Uncle Simon.'

'Hmm.' The deceptively bright eyes peered at her
weakly for a moment, then he shook his head. 'Damn fool
lot they must be,' he declared, and she heard Nick
chuckle.

'I'm in no hurry to marry,' she assured the old man
hastily, and he shook his head.

'Well, they'll be swarming round you like bees round a
honey pot when you're wealthy as well as good-looking,'
he warned her. 'So best you have a man as well off as
yourself, then you'll know why he's marrying you.'

'But, Uncle Simon—'

She was waved to silence by an imperious hand and he
looked across at Nick standing in the doorway. 'Just you

see she doesn't do too much the first time out,' he told him, 'and take good care of her.'

Nick's tip-tilted eyes glowed with laughter, when he saw her surprise at the old man's concern for her. 'I always take good care of her,' he assured him. 'And I shall go on doing so for as long as she allows me to.'

April felt she was being manoeuvred by the two of them into something she did not yet recognize, and she knew she was colouring furiously as she walked across the room towards Nick. 'I don't need anyone to take care of me,' she said, for his ears alone. 'I'm perfectly capable of looking after myself.'

His wide mouth smiled broadly and he put a hand in the middle of her back, drawing her into the hall and closing the door behind them. 'Don't be too sure of that,' he told her softly.

'Of course I can,' she insisted, 'I've been doing it for the past three years.' She walked, small and haughtily indignant, beside him. 'I don't need anyone to take care of me as if I was a baby.'

He laughed softly, his hand still propelling her along. 'I wasn't thinking of treating you like a baby exactly,' he told her. 'Don't be such a spoil-sport.'

'I'm not spoiling anyone's sport,' she retorted, 'but I don't need a guardian, Nick, and especially you.'

He stood for a moment with his hand on the handle of the kitchen door, looking down at her in that enigmatic, slightly sinister way she was beginning to recognize. 'Especially not me?' he echoed. 'Don't be too ready to dismiss me, April, I'm not very easily dismissed.'

April looked at him uneasily and silently for a moment. 'Let's go,' she said at last, 'if we're going.'

It was a beautiful day again and the air smelled hot and summery, fragrant with the perfume of roses as they went through the garden towards the stables and the meadow. It was wonderful weather for riding out in the open country, but there was something more involved beside enjoying herself, as far as April was concerned.

She eyed the sturdy-looking roan apprehensively while Nick saddled him and was ready to cry off her rash promise by the time he turned, ready to help her mount.

'Nick, I—'

'Up you get!'

He bent and cupped his hands for her to step into, but she still hesitated. 'I can't, Nick, please.'

'Nonsense!' He straightened up and stood looking down at her impatiently. 'Dingo's as quiet as a mouse, he won't hurt you.'

She shook her head adamantly, but a moment later squeaked in alarm when she was lifted bodily up into the saddle, her hands automatically reaching for the reins, while the roan seemed prepared to take it all in his stride and merely tossed his head as if in approval. 'O.K.?' Nick looked up at her with a satisfied smile that she was very tempted to remove with a well-placed slap, only she dared not let go the reins.

'No, I'm *not* O.K.,' she told him crossly. 'I'm petrified.'

'Oh, rubbish, you'll soon get used to it again.'

'You're completely callous and unfeeling,' April informed him, wondering if she could manage to dismount without losing too much of her dignity.

'I'm treating you very gently,' he argued. 'I've a feeling you're not nearly as fragile as you look.'

'I don't claim to be fragile,' April retorted, 'but I won't bounce if I fall off this wretched horse either. It's a long way to the ground from here.'

He stood with his hands on his hips, an expression on his face that was as much resigned as impatient. 'You know,' he told her, 'I don't remember you being such a little moaner before.'

'I'm not moaning!'

'Well, it sounds very much like it.'. He walked round and swung himself up on to his own mount, the tall bay that looked as if it could cover a mile with one stride, and she supposed she should thank her lucky stars that he had not seen fit to allocate her that one. 'Ready?' he asked.

'I suppose so,' she allowed, 'but I'm only going as far as the end of the field. Then at least if I fall off I shan't have far to walk home.' She put her heels, very cautiously, to the roan's flanks and almost breathed an audible sigh of relief when he responded slowly and without impatience.

'Take it easy,' Nick advised, and April laughed mirthlessly.

'I intend to,' she assured him.

The rode slowly along the outside of the paddock and when they reached the end of the wooden fence April was prepared to turn back, although she was gaining confidence every minute and Dingo was proving the quietest mount possible. Before she could turn, however, Nick put a hand on the rein and halted her.

'You may as well come the rest of the way to Jordan's now you're this far without incident,' he told her. 'You're doing very well, April.'

'Not that well,' she retorted. 'I'd rather go back, Nick.'

'Oh, come on, cowardy custard,' he jeered. 'Take a chance!'

'No, I – Nick!' He tapped the roan smartly on the rump and started him in the direction of the open country with April clinging on for dear life and desperately trying to remember all Nick had taught her about how to handle a gallop. The roan was doing no more than a steady, reasonable gallop, but to April it seemed like an express train out of control and her hair was lifted and tossed wildly in the breeze they were creating. 'Nick!'

She could just hear the thudding hooves of his mount above the wild tattoo of her heartbeat and knew he was only just behind her. 'Sit up!' The words drifted over to her, but meant nothing, she was too intent on hanging on as best she could.

She was reminded suddenly of another time when she had put the faithful old Cobber into a gallop with the idea of pleasing Nick with her ability, and she remembered how she had ended that run ignominiously in the stream at the bottom of the slope. The same stream that was now looming closer every second, glinting almost malevolently in the sun as if it waited for her down there.

She was surprised that she had managed to stay on so long and thought she must have forgotten less than she imagined. It was more difficult down the lower part of the slope, however, because the increasing angle upset her balance and she had just time to realize what Nick's shouted instructions had meant, and for one last despairing cry before she was flung over the horse's head, legs and arms flying in the most undignified way.

The stream was no deeper now than when she had fallen into it the last time, but it was deep enough to make a resounding splosh when she landed in it, and to soak her clothes through in an uncomfortably short time. Too stunned to move for a moment or two, the first thing she heard was Nick's voice beside her, anxious but still, unbelievably, edged with laughter.

'April! Oh, April my sweet, you're the absolute end!'

'Don't you dare laugh at me,' she told him warningly, 'or I'll—'

'What?' he asked, hauling her to her feet with more

haste than grace. His hands held her tightly while he looked down at her, suddenly and briefly anxious. 'You're not hurt, are you, April?'

She shook her head, almost as much disturbed by the way he was holding her as by the fall. 'No, no, I'm all right, I think.' She tried to look suitably indignant. 'Though it's no thanks to you.'

He laughed, the tip-tilted eyes crinkling at their corners, as he hugged her close for a moment. 'I knew you'd bounce,' he told her, then looked down at her wet clothes. 'Ugh! You *are* soggy!'

'Of course I am,' she retorted. 'What do you expect?' She wriggled free of his hands and looked at the damage. The white trousers were stained and wet and her shoes felt horribly squelchy when she moved.

'It's a very hot today.'

She looked at him, uncomprehending for the moment. 'What's that got to do with it?' she demanded.

'You'll soon dry out in the sun.'

April stared at him. 'Ooh, you unfeeling monster! Is that all you can say?' She put an exploratory hand to the seat of her trousers, the area that had taken most of the ducking, then glared at him angrily. 'It's your fault it happened,' she accused. 'You deliberately stampeded him even though you knew he'd throw me.'

'He didn't throw you,' Nick denied. 'Dingo's never thrown anyone in his life. You fell off. You never did remember to sit back to balance yourself when you go downhill, and I yelled at you too.'

'I didn't know what you were talking about until it was too late. I *told* you I was no horsewoman,' she insisted, almost in tears because she was not only very uncomfortable but had made a fool of herself as well, as she had known she would. 'I'm going back.'

'But we're nearly there now.'

'You don't imagine I'm going to call on anyone like this, do you?' she asked. 'I'm going back, Nick, and—' She stopped suddenly when she realized that they were about to have company. She looked curiously at the tall, fair man who was rapidly approaching, riding at full gallop.

'Is the young lady hurt?' he asked as he came within speaking distance. 'I saw the fall from way over.' There was a genuine concern for her well-being in the quiet, cultured voice and April wondered where she could possibly have seen him before.

He dismounted and came to join them while Nick smiled recognition. 'Hello, Don. April took an extra bath this morning.'

The newcomer had nice grey eyes and they showed more than polite concern; also she thought he recognized her. 'So you *are* Apr – Miss Summers?' he said, extending a hand that engulfed hers completely. 'I'm Donald Jordan – I don't suppose you remember me.'

April smiled, trying to forget the wet, clinging discomfort of her clothes and her undoubted dishevelment. There was something about Donald Jordan that made both seem rather less important suddenly.

The tall, thin boy she only vaguely remembered had grown into a remarkably good-looking man, with thick fair hair in direct contrast to Nick's dark ruggedness. The grey eyes were also flatteringly appreciative despite the effects of her fall, and she found herself feeling less embarrassed and quite flattered.

'Of course I remember you, Mr. Jordan.' She was aware of Nick's dark brows expressing surprise at her *volte-face,* but chose to ignore it.

'I'm flattered!' He had a charming smile. A little reserved perhaps, but genuinely friendly, and he was really very attractive. 'You're terribly wet,' he said concernedly. 'Please won't you come to the house and get dry?'

'Oh, but—'

'Please do,' he urged. 'It's only a very short distance now and you were coming over with Nick anyway, weren't you?'

April nodded, glancing at Nick meaningly. 'That,' she declared darkly, 'was Nick's idea, not mine.'

'Oh? I'm sorry to hear that, I was rather looking forward to seeing you again.'

'I – I didn't quite mean it like that,' April hastened to explain, knowing that inevitably Nick would be finding it all very amusing. 'I know my own limitations as a horse-woman, you see, but Nick stampeded my mount and I had no choice but to come. That's how I came to be thrown.'

'Bad balance,' Nick insisted. 'And Dingo didn't stampede, he merely went at a dignified gallop.'

'Just the same,' Donald Jordan said, frowning, 'it was a damned dangerous thing to do if Miss Summers wasn't used to riding.'

'She did all right until she got to the last piece of the slope,' Nick told him with a grin. 'She never would sit back properly in the saddle.'

'You're not hurt, are you?' Donald Jordan asked her anxiously, and she shook her head, smiling now that someone at least was showing a little sympathy.

It was Nick who helped her to remount and she chose to ignore the suggestively lowered eyelid that commented on the other man's concern for her. 'He's still moon-eyed,' he whispered as he lifted her into the saddle, but she merely stuck her chin in the air and refused to be drawn.

Jordan's was a smaller place altogether than Kinley, but it had a certain functional charm that April thought was practical but still attractive. Unlike Kinley it was a working unit and there were no softening gardens sur-

35

rounding the house, only a few shading trees at the back and the pungent bareness of cobbled yards.

Their host led the way into a low-ceilinged kitchen where a middle-aged woman looked at April curiously, nodding a silent greeting to Nick. 'I can't offer you a change of clothes, I'm afraid,' Donald Jordan explained apologetically. 'This is a bachelor household. Even Mrs. Simms, my housekeeper, comes daily, but you can dry your things while I show Nick the mare he came to see and then perhaps we can have some coffee.'

'It's very kind of you,' April murmured, 'but I'll be O.K., honestly, I'll soon dry.'

'No, no, I insist. You'll catch a chill if you don't get out of those wet things quickly. I'll fetch you a blanket and then get Mrs. Simms to dry your things on the hot tank.'

He was gone only a few minutes and returned with a big red blanket, telling her to give her clothes to the housekeeper when she was ready. 'We'll go and look at the mare,' he told her, while Nick grinned knowingly at her.

'You get on with your strip-tease, April,' he told her. 'We'll be back later.'

'It's only my bottom half that's wet,' she told him shortly, 'though no doubt that is disappointing for you.'

'If you'd done as *I* told you,' he reminded her, 'you wouldn't be wet at all.'

April was soon comfortably settled in an armchair with her lower half wrapped in the blanket, looking round the small but cosy room curiously. There were signs that Donald Jordan was comfortably off, but everything in the room looked as if it was functional first and attractive second. It was a man's house and lacked the womanly touch that would have provided table covers and vases of flowers.

She had been there for perhaps ten or fifteen minutes, looking through an agricultural magazine she had found, when she heard a car draw up outside and looked down at her shrouded lower half in dismay. It would be horribly embarrassing if Donald Jordan was to have a visitor while she was like this, but what could she do about it?

A car door slammed and seconds later there were voices in the hall. Her view from the window was blocked by a brick porch and she had been unable to see who the caller was, but she prayed it would be no one wanting to come in. One voice she distinguished as the housekeeper's and the other was also female, but higher pitched and rather impatient.

April heard the words, 'I'll wait,' and the door opened to admit the visitor.

She stood for a moment on the threshold, adjusting her vision to the dimness of the room after the bright sunshine outside, then she crossed to where April sat, eyes narrowed curiously. The housekeeper had evidently thought it none of her business to make them known to each other and had disappeared into the kitchen again.

'Good afternoon,' April said, politely formal, and feeling more dishevelled than ever in contrast to the other's impeccable elegance.

She was tall, very tall for a woman, and her hair looked white at first in the dimness of the room, but it was in fact ash blonde. Light hazel eyes looked at April coolly and noted not only her untidy, windblown head, but the enshrouding blanket as well. 'Good afternoon.'

Fine brows expressed an opinion without words and April sought for something to say that would explain her presence there in such a state. Perhaps the woman was a close friend of Donald Jordan's, perhaps even more than that, in which case it would be as well to put the record straight as quickly as possible.

'I'm afraid I've had an accident,' she explained, trying to sound off-hand about it. 'My horse threw me and I landed in the stream. Mrs. Simms is drying my clothes.'

'I see.' The sharp eyes still studied her curiously. 'Are you a friend of Donald's?'

'Oh no! That is, not really a friend.' She was unsure just how honest she should be about that. 'I met Mr. Jordan when I stayed at Kinley seven years ago and today's the first time I've seen him since.'

'Kinley?' There was definite interest now. 'You're staying at Kinley?'

April nodded. 'Mr. Carver is my great-uncle.'

'Then you must know—' The sharp eyes glanced out of the far window and there was animation in the rather bored-looking face. 'Is Nick here too?'

April nodded again. 'He's with Mr. Jordan in the yard, they—'

'Hello, Fen.'

The woman swung round so quickly she almost fell and put out a hand to steady herself, a smile of welcome on her face for at least one of the newcomers, and April was pretty sure she knew which it was. Her interest in Nick had been all too obvious, and she went over to him now where he stood with Donald Jordan near the door into the kitchen.

'Nick!' She ignored her host, a fact he seemed to accept as normal, for he came over and stood beside April.

'I didn't expect to find you here,' the woman went on. 'I came to see Donald and—' She shook her head as if the unexpected meeting was more than she could believe. 'I haven't seen you for ages, darling.'

'Not since you decided to try life in the big city,' Nick said quietly, apparently less excited than she was about it. 'Nice to see you back, Fen.' He looked across at April, still a prisoner in her armchair. 'Have you and April met?'

'No.' She seemed uninterested, but Nick made the introduction nevertheless.

'April, this is Fenella Graves. Fen, April Summers, I suppose you could say she's a sort of cousin about fifty times removed. She Pop's great-niece.'

'So I heard before you came in,' Fenella Graves said, obviously not caring at all who April was, especially if she distracted Nick's attention, however briefly.

'I presume you came to see me about the bureau, didn't you, Fenella?' Donald Jordan asked her quietly, determinedly breaking into the reunion, and she nodded.

'I did.'

'Well, you know its price,' Donald told her. 'Are you still interested?'

'Of course I am. You won't come down?' He shook his head adamantly, and the blonde woman sighed. 'Oh, well, I suppose I'll just have to pay you the price you're asking, but you drive a hard bargain, don't you?'

'I'm a business man, Fenella, as well as a farmer,' he told her, 'and I have an expensive hobby.'

'You and your cars!' Fenella Graves sneered. 'I can't think why you have to sell your treasures to pay for them.'

Nick laughed. 'Don doesn't bother so much about what you call treasures, Fen. You covet beautiful furniture like he does fast cars.'

'I like beautiful things,' she admitted, and curled her fingers possessively over his arm. 'I usually get what I want,' she informed him, her voice expressively husky. 'Don't I, darling?'

'Usually,' Nick allowed with a dark smile in April's direction, 'but I wouldn't bank on always doing so, darling.'

39

CHAPTER THREE

IT was something of a surprise when, a couple of days later, April received an invitation to play tennis at Fenella Graves' home, although she realized that she had probably only been included because Nick had been asked and good manners would forbid her exclusion.

'You play, don't you?' he asked, when she commented on it, and she nodded.

'I play, yes. A fair to average game, I suppose. What surprises me is that I've been invited at all. Unless of course,' she added with a glance at him from under her lashes, 'she couldn't do much else if you were going.'

Nick acknowledged the possibility with a knowing grin. 'It could be,' he allowed. 'Although she's asked Donald Jordan too, so I expect you're to be considered *his* partner.'

'While she monopolizes you, I suppose,' April guessed shortly, and saw his brows rise questioningly.

'I expect so,' he said. 'Do you mind?'

April glanced at her great-uncle seated at the other end of the table. The old man appeared not to be listening to their conversation, but she thought he was more interested than he gave the impression of being. 'Of course I don't mind,' she told Nick. 'Why on earth should I?'

Nick shrugged, smiling to himself in a way that April found particularly irritating because she had no idea what caused it. 'I don't know,' he told her. 'Why should you?'

'From what I saw the other day at Jordan's,' she told him, 'I gathered that Miss Graves has a proprietorial interest in you.'

He carefully extracted a peach from the piled-high dish in the centre of the table and gave his attention to it while he spoke. 'Miss Graves has no proprietorial interest in me,' he stated quietly, 'because that implies ownership, and no one owns me, April, no one at all.' He raised his eyes suddenly and held her gaze for a long moment. 'Yet,' he added softly.

She was saved from finding a suitable answer to that last enigmatic statement by her great-uncle. 'Fenella Graves,' he declared authoritatively, 'is exactly like her mother was. She knows exactly what she wants and she'll stop at nothing to make sure she gets it. She's a very determined woman.'

'Did you know her mother, Uncle Simon?' April asked, not quite knowing why she was so surprised at the discovery. She did not remember hearing anything of Fenella Graves during her last visit, but perhaps then she had not moved in the same circles as Nick.

'I knew *of* her,' the old man agreed. 'The Graves and the Bennetts have lived around here for as long as I can remember. Mary Bennett was a woman who knew her own mind and she set her cap at George Graves from the time she was a young girl, and eventually married him. He was a very wealthy young man and her father was the village poacher.'

'Oh – I see.'

'What Pop is telling you,' Nick informed her with a wry grin, 'is that Fen's mother married above herself and got rich.'

'She set her mind on marrying money,' the old man said sharply, 'and her daughter's prepared to do the same, unless I misjudge her.'

Nick laughed softly, but it was difficult to tell whether the accusation disturbed him or not since he kept his eyes

41

carefully lowered. 'If she is,' he said, 'she's a bit off target at the moment, Pop.'

'If she's got her sights on you, she isn't off target,' his stepfather retorted sharply. 'You'll be a rich man when I'm gone, Nick, and she must know it.'

'Of course she knows it, or at least guesses it,' Nick allowed, 'but I think you're taking it all too seriously, Pop, and anyway, Fen has plenty of money of her own without marrying me for mine.' He smiled at the old man affectionately, and April marvelled, not for the first time, at the bond between them. There was no blood-tie between them, but they were closer than many a natural father and his son. Nick laughed, shaking his head. 'I can manage Fenella, don't you worry.'

'I hope you can,' his stepfather said brusquely.

Nick turned his attention to April again. 'What about it, April, are you coming to Fen's for tea and tennis?'

She had a sudden desire to giggle, hearing it put like that. It reminded her of all she had heard about vicarage tea-parties and a more leisurely age. 'It sounds madly Victorian the way you put it,' she told him. 'I shall have to come out of sheer curiosity.'

'*And* to see Don Jordan again.'

His gaze challenged her to deny it, and April lifted her chin, smiling. 'Of course to meet Don Jordan again,' she agreed. 'I think he's *very* attractive.'

When she saw their neighbour again a couple of days later, April thought Donald Jordan looked even more attractive in his tennis gear of white shorts and shirt. Although, for all his outdoor tan, his fairness paled beside Nick, similarly dressed.

Donald had seen them coming, being ahead of them, and he came across to open the car door for April before Nick could leave his own seat, looking at her with an

42

appreciative smile. 'April! It's good to see you again.'

She had met him once more since the day she took her ignominious tumble into the stream, and he had taken immediate advantage of her invitation to use her christian name.

'Hello, Donald.' She was, she admitted, giving only half her attention to him once they had exchanged greetings, being busy speculating on Fenella Graves' choice of dress for the occasion.

Evidently she took her tennis very seriously, for she wore tailored shorts and a quite masculine shirt, both of which were functional but not very flattering. April's own attire was much more feminine although perhaps not so practical, but she had been obliged to improvise from what she already had in her wardrobe, and hoped to borrow a racquet from their hostess, having none of her own with her.

The short white dress showed off her slim legs to perfection and left her arms bare to the sun which she hoped would soon give her a tan. Her short hair was further controlled by a ribbon that tied it back from her face and gave her rather a little-girl look. Nick, before they left Kinley, had told her that she looked devastating, but she had long since decided to take Nick's compliments with a pinch of salt.

Donald Jordan's expression, however, showed that he shared much the same opinion and he retained his hold on her hand for some seconds after it was necessary. 'You look incredibly lovely,' he told her when Nick had gone out of earshot in company with their hostess. 'So lovely I could—' He stopped short suddenly, looking vaguely sheepish as if he had said too much. 'I'm – I'm sorry, April,' he apologized. 'I shouldn't be so pushing so soon. You'll think I'm as—'

He did not finish the sentence, but a brief, telling

43

glance in Nick's direction made his meaning plain enough
and April smiled. 'As bad as Nick?' she guessed, and
shook her head. 'Please don't apologize, Donald, no
woman minds being told how nice she looks.'

'And I really do mean it,' he assured her, as they followed the other two along a gravel path towards the
tennis court. 'I've always thought how lovely you were,
April.'

She smiled up at him, liking his quiet, earnest but
somewhat reticent manner which she found such a contrast to Nick's unquenchable self-confidence. Donald, she
thought, would never indulge in idle compliments as Nick
did, and immediately scolded herself for comparing
them.

'I'm surprised you still remembered me,' she told him
lightly. 'I was only a schoolgirl when I was here
before.'

'You were lovely,' he insisted, 'and I adored you all
those four months you were here. I was inconsolable
when you left to go back to London, though of course I
knew you had eyes only for Nick.'

April pulled a wry face. 'Oh, please don't remind me of
that,' she begged. 'I've been through it all with Nick and I
could curl up and die with embarrassment when I think
of what an idiot I must have seemed then.'

'Not at all,' he declared loyally. 'It was understandable,
although I hated him at the time. He's very attractive to
the women, and he takes advantage of it. I can't really
blame him.'

April looked at him curiously. 'How?' she asked, and
saw him blink uncomprehendingly. 'How does he take
advantage of it?' she enlarged.

Donald shrugged. 'Oh, you know,' he said, offhand,
and obviously not prepared to enlighten her further.

She said no more until they joined Nick and Fenella,

44

waiting for them on the court, but she had been shown a side of Nick she had not known before, although she supposed she should have suspected it. Nick was a man that most women would find irresistible and he would also not hesitate to take advantage of it, as Donald had said.

The tennis court was in a beautiful setting, the garden being planted with every conceivable tree and shrub and with neat flower beds bordering the gravel paths. There was surely no need for Fenella Graves to marry for money when she was so obviously wealthy in her own right, as Nick had pointed out, and it was more likely that her reason for behaving as she did with Nick was for the reason that Donald had mentioned rather than her great-uncle's version.

'Ready for the fray?' April started almost guiltily when he spoke close to her ear, and she nodded, wondering how rusty her tennis was in comparison to her companions'.

'I just hope I don't let everybody down,' she said, and Nick laughed softly.

'You'd better not,' he warned her, 'or I shall refuse to take you anywhere else.'

She would have replied, indignantly, but he was already walking away from her again and she could do no more than glare after him resentfully.

April partnered Donald, who was a strong vigorous player, but not particularly expert, and she was dismayed to find how tired the game made her after so long without playing. She did as well as she could, however, but it was soon evident that she and Donald were no match for two far better players, and they went down miserably to Nick and Fenella in the first two sets.

'It's now or never,' Donald told her, as they began the third set. 'And I rather think it's never.'

How right he was was proved in a dismally short time and April could not help feeling that it was mostly her

45

fault. No matter what she tried to do, it seemed, if Nick was concerned in any way, she was fated to fail miserably and she felt an unreasoning resentment for his superiority.

Her attempt at riding a horse had, in the first instance, proved a fiasco, although she had managed rather more successfully since. And now she had shown herself embarrassingly incompetent on the tennis court, especially in contrast to Fenella Graves. Obviously she was not cut out to be a sportswoman and Nick should realize it and make allowances.

They all four gratefully settled in the shade for a traditional English tea, and it all seemed so peaceful and slightly unreal that April felt she was somewhere back in the nineteenth century, cut off from the rest of the world by the tall, shadowy trees. Only the three pairs of shorts and her own brief skirt spoiled the illusion, and for a while she was content to forget her own inadequacies and enjoy her tea.

It was when Nick decided to partner April after tea that things started to go really wrong and the atmosphere of the party grew much less friendly, so that April wondered why he had chosen to make the suggestion when he must have known quite well the effect it would have on his former partner.

Fenella disliked the idea and made no secret of it, but Nick was adamant, pointing out that it would be a far more even match with the two stronger players divided. It was evident when they started playing again that the change had certainly evened things up a bit, but partnering Nick made April more than ever aware of her shortcomings and her play was, if anything, worse than it had been in the first match.

For the umpteenth time she returned the ball into the net instead of clearing it and Nick frowned at her blackly

46

as they waited for Fenella's service. 'One more like that and I'll wallop you with my racquet,' he threatened.

April looked at him reproachfully. 'I'm trying,' she told him.

It was an extra energetic leap for the ball that sent her, a few minutes later, sprawling across the court with her left foot doubled under her painfully. She wondered for a second if anyone had even noticed her fall, and then Nick was on one knee beside her, lifting her and straightening out the leg from under her.

'April!'

He sounded anxious, but April convinced herself that he was more concerned with her spoiling the game. He held her so that she could not have got to her feet even if she'd tried, and he picked up the injured foot gently.

'Does it hurt very much?' he asked, when she winced.

'Yes.' She bit her lip, the ankle throbbing painfully. 'It – it hurts like blazes.'

He nodded, as if it was exactly what he expected, and even now she could marvel at his self-confidence. There was no hesitation or doubt about his actions, he looked as if he knew exactly what he was doing, and she was convinced he did. 'Then you'd better not stand on it,' he told her brusquely.

Fenella was standing beside him, a faint curl to her lips, while Donald knelt on the other side of April his eyes anxious, but much less sure of what he could do to help. 'Had we better get a doctor?' he suggested. 'It's beginning to swell rather badly.'

Nick's strong fingers felt gently round her ankle. 'Can you move it at all?' he asked her. 'Try to if you can, I know it hurts, but just see if you can.'

'I'll – I'll try,' she gasped, making an effort and biting on her lip when she at last managed to get the ankle to

47

move, however slightly, wiggling her toes for good measure. She noted Nick's nod of satisfaction with mixed feelings. 'I'm glad you're pleased,' she told him, near to tears with pain and humiliation. It seemed she was destined to make a fool of herself in front of Donald Jordan, and it was all due to Nick, or so she told herself.

'I'm pleased it isn't broken,' he informed her. 'A cold compress will do for the moment, then when I get you home I have something that will fix you up in no time.'

'I – I don't need a cold compress,' she denied, but he merely pursed his lips, as if tantrums were only what he expected of her.

'I really think we should get a doctor for—' Donald began, only to be interrupted impatiently by their hostess.

'I don't agree,' Fenella said shortly, glaring at April as if she suspected her of deliberate sabotage. 'It's only a slight sprain and nothing to make a fuss about.'

'It must be very painful,' Donald protested, holding April's hand protectively and making her feel more tearful than ever.

'Well, come up to the house and I'll get someone to put a cold bandage on it for you,' Fenella told her, sighing resignedly. 'I suppose it's useless to try and go on with the game anyway.' She sounded so grudgingly ungracious about it that April could have curled up and died on the spot with misery and embarrassment.

'I'm – I'm sorry, Fenella.' It was hard to apologize to so ungracious a hostess, but April supposed something was due. After all, she had been responsible for disrupting the game and more or less spoiling the rest of the afternoon.

Fenella made no answer but turned away, obviously disgusted with the whole incident, while April found herself scooped up as if she weighed no more than a child,

instinctively putting an arm round Nick's shoulders as he lifted her.

'I could have—' Donald began, but Nick had possession and was evidently not prepared to relinquish it.

'There's no need,' he told Donald. 'I can manage her.'

'I can walk,' April insisted, hoping he wouldn't take her at her word, for the injured ankle was throbbing more painfully than ever, and Nick was quite capable of carrying her.

'Don't be an idiot!' he told her bluntly.

'Oh, you—' She felt the first tear already trembling on her eyelid and blinked it away determinedly. Her hand was clenched where it rested on his shoulder and she was very tempted to hit him with it, hard.

'You can't walk on a sprained ankle,' he told her, a wry grin recognizing her temptation, 'so sit still and try to use your head for once. And *don't*,' he added with a short laugh, 'hit me with that fist, or I'll sling you into the rhododendrons!'

The party broke up on something of an anti-climax and April sat, small and miserable, beside Nick on the way home, feeling as if she was being held responsible for everything. If only Nick had not made that threat to her about persistently netting the ball she would have never overreached herself in an effort to do better and it would never have happened.

He glanced at her as they drove along, and she thought he was smiling, but she refused to look at him long enough to be sure. 'Are you sitting there brooding?' he asked. 'Feeling sorry for yourself?'

She did not reply at once, finding no words to express how she felt at his lack of sympathy. The old Nick, she felt sure, would never have been so callously unfeeling if she had been hurt. 'My – my foot hurts,' she managed at last, and sounded very lost and forlorn.

'I expect it does.' A hand reached over, unexpectedly, and covered hers for a brief moment of sympathy. 'Never mind, little 'un, I'll soon fix it when we get home.'

'I'm – I'm sorry I spoiled your afternoon.'

He laughed. 'You seem destined to be brought home the worse for wear, don't you?' he asked, as if the idea was more amusing than regrettable.

'I don't think it's funny, Nick.' Anger was beginning to take over from self-pity and she glared at him. 'I seem to make a fool of myself all too often when I'm with you, and I don't think it's very funny.'

'You're saying it's my fault?'

'No, of course not.'

'You're just accident-prone,' he told her. 'I shall have to take better care of you or I shall have Pop after me.'

April flushed at the suggestion that she was incapable of taking care of herself. 'I've told you, Nick, I don't need a guardian, least of all you.'

'I remember,' he said, 'and this afternoon you've proved how wrong you are, haven't you?'

'But I'm not a baby,' she insisted. 'I'm just not a – a sporty type.'

'Obviously,' he chuckled. 'I'd better see that you don't get involved in anything more than a quiet game of cards in future.'

'You sound as if you think I'm some sort of a – a moron,' she accused, and looked at him curiously when he frowned.

'I think no such thing,' he averred, quite serious. 'I suppose I shouldn't tease you so, should I, April?'

She scarcely knew how to reply to that and for a moment or so she said nothing. It was only when they turned into the driveway at Kinley that she found the courage to say what she thought, and wondered if she was asking for further trouble, even as she spoke.

'I – I don't really mind if you tease me, Nick. I – I sup-pose I am a bit touchy sometimes, but you always—' She stopped then and bit her lip, knowing that it was only because of the way she had once felt about him that she was so vulnerable to his taunts.

He stopped the car at the front door and lifted her out of the car, and she was close enough to him to see the lines at the corners of those intriguing eyes as he carried her into the house. 'Nick—'

'Hmm?'

'You don't blame me for this afternoon, do you?'

He smiled, and she was close enough to see the glitter of laughter when he looked down at her. 'Of course I don't,' he told her. 'You couldn't help falling over your feet.'

Uncle Simon looked surprised to see them home so early, but was unexpectedly sympathetic about her mis-fortune. 'Better leave it to Nick to take care of it,' he told her when his stepson went off to fetch something that he assured her would ease the pain in no time.

'I don't seem to have much option,' April said wryly, dumped unceremoniously on the settee in the sitting-room, and the old man nodded.

'That's right, my girl, you haven't.'

It was only minutes later that Nick returned carrying a bottle of what was presumably some kind of liniment, for it smelled foully strong and felt hot and oily when he rubbed it in. He perched on the settee beside her and she wondered what sort of magic formula he was using that he had such confidence in its healing powers.

His fingers were strong and gentle and she began to feel the effect almost at once, the ankle felt much less painful as he worked in the oily liniment. 'How does it feel?' he asked, glancing up after a while.

'Much better – I think.'

He grinned. 'You'll soon feel the benefit,' he told her. 'This is very good stuff. I had a sprained wrist last year and it was back in action in no time at all, thanks to this stuff.'

April wrinkled her nose. 'It smells terrible,' she said. 'What is it, Nick?' He did not answer, but merely smiled in a way that made her immediately suspicious, and glanced across at the old man. 'Nick?'

'Something that's doing your ankle good,' he told her, obviously being evasive. 'Beyond that it doesn't matter, does it?'

April too looked at her great-uncle and surprised an uncharacteristic gleam of amusement in the weak, blue eyes. 'Uncle Simon,' she pleaded, 'what has he put on my ankle?'

'Horse liniment,' the old man informed her, 'but don't worry, it works quite well on humans too.'

'*Horse* liniment!' April looked down at her ankle, pungently shiny, and then at Nick. 'But—'

'But nothing,' Nick retorted. 'I told you I used it on my own wrist, so it won't do you any harm.'

'Well, I hope not,' she told him anxiously. 'I'm not sure I relish being treated like Dingo or one of the other horses. I suppose if I'd broken my leg you'd have shot me?'

Nick stood up, his tip-tilted eyes glowing with malicious laughter. 'Quite likely,' he agreed solemnly. 'It's kindest in the long run.'

Instructed to keep off her ankle for a day or two, April sat in a chair in the garden, her bandaged foot propped up on a stool. It was warm enough to make her feel heavy-eyed and sleepy and she was almost over the brink into sleep when Mrs. Widgeon came through from the house with the information that Donald Jordan had arrived to see her.

A hasty check on her hair and April looked up with a

smile at the visitor's anxious face. 'April!' he came and sat beside her on another chair provided by Mrs. Widgeon, putting down a bunch of flowers he carried and reaching for her hands as he sat down. 'How are you?'

April wrinkled her nose. 'Smelly,' she told him. 'It's much less painful, though, thank you, Donald, so I'm prepared to suffer the awful smell if it works. As long as you don't mind.'

'Of course I don't,' he assured her, and sniffed deeply. 'It smells like horse liniment, is it?'

April made a face. 'So Nick told me; *after* he'd put it on, of course. He swears by it, apparently it healed a sprained wrist of his last year.'

'I remember,' he said. 'But I've used it myself too. It's very good stuff, but somehow the idea of using it on you doesn't seem quite – well, quite right.'

She laughed appreciatively at the implied compliment. 'It's not exactly Chanel Number Five,' she agreed, 'but if it works I don't care *too* much what it smells like.'

'I brought you some flowers.' He reached down under the chair and retrieved the bouquet of flowers. 'Though it's a bit like carrying coals to Newcastle, I suppose, with all those roses behind you.'

'The roses are beautiful, aren't they?' she agreed, and lifted the bunch of heavy-headed stocks to her nose. 'But these smell gorgeous, Donald, you must have known I needed something to counteract that liniment.'

'I didn't see exactly how you hurt yourself,' Donald said after a moment or two. 'You were already on the ground when I saw you and I'm afraid I daren't risk jumping the net or I'd have come a cropper too – besides, Nick was already in charge.'

He sounded almost bitter about it, but at the same time resigned, as if he was used to the situation and saw it as inevitable. 'I was trying too hard to make up for my bad play,' April explained ruefully. 'I tried to return that backhand of Fenella Graves' and I overreached myself and went sprawling. It was most undignified and you must think I'm a complete idiot.'

'I think nothing of the sort,' Donald denied earnestly. 'I'm only sorry I couldn't do anything to help, but there was nothing I *could* do.'

'Of course there wasn't,' April reassured him. 'There was little anyone could do, it was just a stupid accident pure and simple. Was Miss Graves very angry about my spoiling her party?'

He shrugged, and passed an opinion as surely as if he had spoken. 'How could she be angry?' he said. 'It wasn't your fault, it was just bad luck.'

'Like falling off my horse into a stream,' April told him ruefully, pulling a face. 'I have to face the fact, I'm afraid, Donald, I'm just not a sporting type, although Nick insists on trying to make me into one.'

'You do seem to have been very unlucky,' he agreed. 'You must take more care, April, or you'll be seriously injured one of these days.'

'Oh, I don't think it's that bad,' April laughed, trying to make light of it. 'But from now on, I don't care what threats and inducements Nick makes, I'm not taking on anything I feel I can't handle.'

'Threats?' He looked worried at the idea as he took up an only half-serious statement. 'You mean Nick actually *makes* you do these things?'

'Well – no, of course not, not really,' she admitted, not prepared to see Nick made an out-and-out villain, although she had been thinking of him in that role in her own mind. She smiled to show that she was not taking it seriously and pulled a doleful face. 'But he did threaten to whack me with his racquet if I netted the ball just once more.'

She had not expected to be taken seriously, especially as she had laughed about it, but Donald, it seemed, was not treating it so lightly and he frowned. 'He had no right to do that,' he said sternly, and took her hands in his again. 'I didn't realize, April.'

April shook her head, appalled that he should be taking it all so seriously. 'But he didn't mean it, of course,' she hastened to assure him.

Donald frowned still. 'I should hope not,' he told her. 'If I thought he did, I'd have something to say to him, make no mistake about that.'

CHAPTER FOUR

IT was not really a surprise to April when, the following evening, Donald again came to see her and she welcomed him delightedly, although she thought her great-uncle was less enthusiastic about the visit judging by his frown when Mrs. Widgeon announced his arrival. Nick merely raised a brow and smiled at her knowingly.

'I hope I'm not intruding,' Donald said, when he was shown into the sitting-room, 'but as you aren't able to get about much, April, I wondered if you'd like to come for a ride.'

The old man's frown deepened as he waited for April to answer. 'I – I'd love to come, Donald, thank you.'

'In one of your noisy monstrosities?' the old man asked brusquely, and Donald looked rather taken aback.

'It's a very fast car, Mr. Carver, but it's safe enough,' he assured him. 'I promise you that.'

'Hmm. Car's only as safe as its driver,' Uncle Simon retorted, evidently not to be convinced. 'My niece already has a sprained ankle, I wouldn't take very kindly to having her brought home with something worse.'

'Oh no, of course not!' Donald looked anxious. 'I'm a very careful driver, Mr. Carver, I assure you, and I shall be extra careful with April in the car.'

'Hmm!'

'Oh, Uncle Simon,' April objected, 'I'm sure Donald's an excellent driver and you have no need to worry.' She glanced up at her visitor, smiling encouragingly, and he nodded.

'No need at all,' he assured the old man earnestly.

'And I could do with a change of air and scenery,' April

told him, forgetting for the moment that she had declined a similar offer from Nick earlier in the day. A second later however, a raised brow and a discreet cough reminded her, and she hastily looked away again after catching his eye. 'It's much too warm to need a coat,' she added hurriedly, 'so I'm ready when you are, Donald.'

He watched her anxiously as she struggled to her feet and tried out her weight on the injured foot. 'Just give me time to hobble out to the car,' she laughed.

'Can't I carry you?' he asked anxiously, but April shook her head.

'No, I can manage perfectly well, thank you.'

'If you're sure.' He hovered anxiously as she took an unsteady step in the direction of the door. 'I could quite easily carry you, April, if you'd—'

She shook her head firmly, took another step, then squeaked protestingly when she was lifted off her feet and carried to the door. 'Nick! Nick, put me down, I can manage!'

'I told you to keep off it for a few days,' he reminded her, 'but telling you is a waste of time, isn't it?'

'I object to being told what to do!' She circled an arm round his neck as he carried her through to the hall. 'I can manage.'

'And take all night getting to the door,' he retorted with a grin.

'Oh, I see, so that's it.' She put on a haughty face and looked down her nose at him. 'You can't wait to get me out of the house, is that it?'

He crossed the hall with her, followed by Donald, who looked as if he found the incident very distasteful. 'Something like that,' he agreed with a grin.

'Sometimes I hate you,' she informed him solemnly, looking at the rugged, expressive face, and could not repress a smile.

'You deserve it for refusing to come out with me,' he told her, and laughed softly, calling back over his shoulder to Donald before she could reply, 'Where shall I dump her, Don? In the boot?'

'Don't you dare!' It was April who answered him while Donald hurriedly opened the passenger door, as if he feared he might carry out his threat.

'Whew!' She was deposited in the front seat and, as her arm slid from round his neck, his lips brushed warmly against hers before he released her. 'Have a nice trip,' he whispered, and lowered one eyelid over a wicked gleam.

'Thanks, I will,' she told him lightly, trying to ignore the way her heart was behaving and the warm flush in her cheeks. 'Don't wait up for me!'

Donald drove in silence for a moment or two, as if he was still resenting the way the initiative had been taken away from him, and April glancing at him curiously, thought his friendship with Nick was not a very close one. He might, she guessed, not only dislike Nick but secretly envy him too.

'It's a lovely evening.' Her words seemed to rouse him out of his mood and he turned and looked at her briefly.

'Lovely,' he agreed, with a smile.

'It's very good of you to think about me being a prisoner in the house,' she told him. 'I appreciate it, Donald.'

He relaxed more now, and flicked her another smile over his shoulder. 'It's as much for my own benefit as yours,' he told her. 'Probably more so. I wanted to take you out, April, and this was a heaven-sent opportunity. A marvellous excuse to ask you.'

April frowned at him curiously. 'Do you *need* an excuse?' she asked.

He negotiated a corner carefully before he answered. 'Of course I do,' he told her. 'It takes nerve to move in on Nick Lawton's territory.'

She stared at him for a moment, her mind racing in all sorts of directions at once, then she shook her head. 'I think you have the wrong idea altogether, Donald,' she told him. 'I can go out with whoever I please. It has nothing to do with Nick.'

'No?'

'No!' April insisted firmly.

He glanced at her briefly and she thought he was puzzled or possibly even disbelieving in the first instance. 'I'm sorry if I got it wrong,' he said.

'You very definitely have,' April insisted.

He was silent for a moment, then he smiled dryly. 'Well, at least your – Mr. Carver wasn't very pleased to see me,' he said.

April laughed. 'Oh, Uncle Simon's bark is much worse than his bite,' she told him.

He was silent for a while while he drove the big, powerful car expertly through the narrow lanes. 'Do you still – idolize Nick?' he asked, and sensed almost at once that he had perhaps been indiscreet to ask that so bluntly. 'I'm sorry,' he said. 'I shouldn't have asked you that.'

'There's no need to apologize,' April assured him. 'The answer is simple enough. No, I don't still nurse my schoolgirl crush for Nick, it was just that – a schoolgirl crush. But,' she added cautiously, 'I can see that he'd appeal to quite a lot of women, especially now he's that much older.'

'Oh, he does that all right,' Donald declared, and confirmed her earlier suspicions that he was probably envious of Nick. 'He makes the most of his chances too, but I shouldn't be surprised if he's met his match in Fenella.'

April absorbed that for a moment, unwilling to give the impression that she was too interested, but undeniably curious about Nick's relationship with Fenella Graves. 'Are they very – close?' she asked.

'Pretty close, by all appearances,' Donald said, and glanced at her curiously. 'Don't you know?'

April shook her head. 'No. I didn't even know that Nick had a reputation as – well, a reputation, and I'd never even heard of Fenella Graves until that day I saw her at your farm. Uncle Simon says they've lived round here for generations, but I've just never heard of her.'

'They never mixed much locally when Mrs. Graves was alive,' Donald informed her. 'It's only since her mother died about a year ago that Fenella's come into prominence as a social butterfly. Then three months ago she went off to try her wings in London, but I suppose she couldn't settle and she came back.' He flicked her a speculative look over one shoulder. 'I suspect Nick had quite a lot to do with her coming back,' he said.

'Quite likely.' She hoped she sounded off-hand enough. She disliked the idea of Nick and Fenella Graves, for no good reason that she could think of except that the blonde woman was one of the few people she had ever taken an instant dislike to. Probably, she thought, ruefully, they deserved each other. 'She seems to consider that she has first call on his time,' she added, and Donald laughed shortly.

'As I said,' he told her, 'I wouldn't be at all surprised if he hasn't met his match in Fenella.'

The countryside was beginning to look dusty and a little tired after a long, hot spell, but it was still a welcome change from town and April enjoyed speeding along in the car with the wind whipping back her hair and bringing heightened colour to her cheeks. Although they were travelling quite fast, she suspected that the powerful car was capable of much greater speeds and that Donald usually drove much faster than he was now.

She remembered at the farm, his brief and rather acid exchange with Fenella about his expensive hobby, and found it difficult now, as then, to match what little she knew of Donald's character with a liking for fast cars. It would have been a passion easier to attribute to Nick.

'Would you like to stop somewhere for a while?' Donald asked suddenly, breaking into her reverie, and April smiled. 'Mmm. Why not? It's a lovely evening.'

'At a pub, or somewhere out here?'

She glanced at him before answering. 'Out here somewhere suits me fine,' she told him. 'If it's O.K. with you, that is. But stop at a pub by all means, if you'd rather.'

He shook his head, taking the car up on to a wide grass verge that gave a magnificent view of the countryside. 'I don't usually, when I'm driving,' he said. 'I just didn't know if you—' He shook his head hastily, suddenly embarrassed, and reached over to open the car door and admit a little more cool air.

April looked at him for the moment it took him to lean across her to the door, and wondered if she had interpreted his doubts correctly. His good-looking face was still remarkably fair-skinned despite his outdoor life, and the nice grey eyes always seemed to look a little anxious.

'You weren't sure if I'd want to stop out here in the middle of nowhere with you, is that it?' she suggested softly, and shook her head when he looked quite startled at the accuracy of her guess.

'I wouldn't have blamed you,' he assured her earnestly. 'It is rather a time-worn situation, isn't it?'

'I suppose so.' She looked out at the lengthening shadows in the valley below them and felt suddenly and inexplicably romantic.

It was beautiful country and they must be miles from anywhere at the moment. It was, as Donald had said, a time-worn situation and no doubt Nick would have made much different use of it in Donald's place. Nick! She pulled herself up sharply, startled to find Nick intruding into the scene. And Donald too must have been similarly plagued, for his words betrayed a train of thought like her own.

'I expect *Nick* would have made the most of his chances by now,' he remarked, and April frowned. Nick, it seemed, was destined to haunt them.

'I don't know what Nick would have done,' she told him shortly. 'And quite frankly, I don't particularly care.'

'There you are, you see,' he said ruefully. '*I* always seem to say the wrong thing.'

Determined to change the subject, April swung her feet out on to the grass. 'I'd love to go to the edge of the rise,' she told him. 'May we?'

He was out of the car in an instant, and hesitated only briefly before lifting her into his arms, although she protested she was quite well able to walk as long as she had something or somebody to hold on to. 'Better safe than sorry,' he told her. 'And you're no weight at all to carry.'

He set her down gently on the grassy top of the slope and sat himself down beside her, while April breathed in the warm, summery air and smiled. 'I never get tired of the country,' she said. 'Especially after living in town.'

'You *are* going back to town?' he asked, looking down at the grass tuft under his fingers.

April looked puzzled, something in his voice making her curious. 'Oh yes, I expect so, sooner or later. After all, I'm not a wealthy woman yet, and I hope I won't be for some time yet. Besides, I like my job, even if it isn't very grand. I'm a commercial artist,' she added.

The grey eyes looked at her seriously as usual, but he smiled for a moment. 'I hadn't realized you were talented as well as lovely,' he said, and she shook her head in denial of such lavish praise. She had no illusions about her own limitations.

'Not all that talented,' she confessed. 'I'm only a very small cog in a very big wheel, Donald.'

'Have you given it up to come to Kinley?'

'For the time being.' She could still not have explained exactly what had possessed her to act so impulsively. 'Uncle Simon asked me to come and stay with him for two or three months and I – well, I just acted on impulse and came. I'm rather like that, I'm afraid,' she added ruefully. 'And I can't for the life of me think why it had to be for so long.' She laughed, remembering her uncle's reason for asking her to Kinley and her own initial surprise at hearing it. 'He wants to give me the once-over,' she told him.

'The once-over?' He looked surprised and then so shocked suddenly that she wondered what kind of a man he thought her uncle was.

'That's right.' She laughed again. 'See what he was getting for his money, in a way, I suppose.'

Donald stared at her as if he fully expected her to share his own feelings and was rather disgusted because she didn't. 'My God, April,' he said at last. 'I – I suspected something of the sort, but after you said – well, I thought I must have been mistaken.'

'Mistaken? Mistaken about what, Donald?'

'Why – the reason he asked you here.' He shook his head slowly. 'I – I wonder he has the nerve to be so blatantly open about it, though.'

'Well, why shouldn't he be?' April asked, more puzzled

63

than ever. 'I suppose it's logical from his point of view, although I must admit I didn't quite see it in the same light at first.'

'But— Don't you *mind*?'

She shrugged, still wondering at his making quite so much of it. 'No, I don't really mind. I suppose it's a reasonable precaution in the circumstances.'

'But it's – it's monstrous!' He was still far more angry than she thought he had need to be, and she looked at him curiously.

'I don't quite understand,' she said slowly. 'Why is it so awful for Uncle Simon to want to know what sort of a woman I've grown into before he decides to leave me half his fortune. He wanted to know me better first, and in the circumstances, I can see his point.'

'Leave you—' Donald stared at her for a moment, then hastily averted his eyes and plucked at the dry summer grass beside him.

'What other reason did you think he had, Donald?' He did not reply, obviously far too embarrassed to voice his own interpretation. 'Donald?'

'Oh – none, I suppose,' he said. 'I'm sorry.'

'It must have been *some*thing to make you sound so – so angry,' she insisted, and reached over to still the restless fingers plucking at the grass. 'Tell me, Donald.'

He shook his head, turning his hand to enfold hers. 'No, I'd rather not.'

'Please!'

For a moment he said nothing, then he looked up and met her eyes uneasily. 'I should have known from the way you spoke earlier,' he confessed, 'but I thought – well, I thought your uncle had – had plans for you.'

'Plans?'

He nodded, his fingers tight as they curled over hers. 'Plans for you and Nick,' he said.

'For me and— Oh no!'

'I can see now that I was very much out,' he said hastily, 'and I'm sorry, April.'

'You *are* – very much out,' she declared firmly, but as she looked out once more over the quiet, sunlit scene below them, she felt the first cool shiver of evening flutter against her spine, and held on to his hand, wondering just how wrong he had been, or if it was she who had been too naïve to realize that there was something more behind her great-uncle's invitation.

It was the following day that April noticed a distinctly uncomfortable itching sensation under the bandage on her ankle. It had been a long, hot day and the injured foot had been paining her more than usual because she had been reckless enough to try and walk downstairs on it that morning, and almost had another fall.

Sympathy had been in short supply, especially from Nick. In fact she had been informed that it served her right for trying to do too much too soon, so that for the rest of the day she had suffered not only from a throbbing pain in her ankle, but from a feeling of being ill-used as well.

Although she had done nothing more strenuous than sit in a chair all day, it had been so hot she was feeling sticky and irritable and miserable enough to cry in sheer self-pity. The maddening itch which now added to her troubles was the very last straw, and she thought she would risk her amateur doctor's wrath and remove the bandage to discover the cause.

She really felt ridiculously guilty as she unwound the yards of cotton bandage and stared at her foot in dismay a few moments later at what was revealed. The swelling had certainly gone down considerably, although the ankle ached, but she was aghast at the angry red rash that looked even worse against a background of bruises.

'Oh no!' April was one of those people to whom any skin blemish is immediately exaggerated into something utterly unbearable and she gazed at the inflamed ankle in something akin to horror.

She sat there for several moments, almost willing the new discomfort to disappear before her eyes, feeling tears of self-pity blurring her vision before rolling dismally down her cheeks. It really was the last straw, she thought, and, what was worse, she would probably be told that *this* served her right too.

She was still sitting staring at the offending rash and with tears rolling down her face, when her great-uncle came into the room a few minutes later, having convinced herself that not only was the rash some hideous disease, but that she was destined to experience one unpleasant incident after another at Kinley. She should never have come, she told herself, and she would leave again as soon as she was fit to travel, in the meantime she was further plagued by this ghastly rash, and if she felt like crying like a baby then she would, regardless of what anyone thought of her.

'April!' The old man came over to her, laying a hand on her shoulder. 'What on earth's the matter, girl?'

April raised her face, and her voice had a quavery sound when she at last managed to answer. 'It's my foot,' she wailed. 'Look at it!'

Old Simon's weak eyes peered curiously, then he shook his head. 'I can't see very well,' he told her, 'but it looks inflamed. It's probably that near fall you had this morning, I'll go and ask Nick to take a look at it, and see what he thinks.'

'I don't care *what* he thinks,' April protested. 'It has nothing to do with my coming downstairs this morning, and it *isn't* my fault.'

He said nothing for a moment, but merely looked at her steadily in a way that reminded her of Nick, then he went to the door again, his stick thudding softly on the carpet. 'Nick had better see it,' he said. 'His eyesight is better than mine.'

'No!' She sounded utterly in despair. Her ankle was throbbing painfully, apart from anything else, and she felt more sorry for herself than ever. Nick was the last person she wanted to see at that moment.

'Don't be foolish, my girl!' The old man sounded firm, and she subsided miserably against the cushions, hearing voices in the hall a few minutes later.

It was only seconds before the door opened again and Nick came in alone, while April hastily rubbed her eyes, refusing to show tears in front of him. He said nothing until he had lifted her bodily from the armchair she occupied and put her on the settee so that he could perch on it too.

'Now,' he said, very businesslike, 'what's wrong?'

April said nothing, but she knew he was looking at her tear-stained face and woebegone expression. He lifted her foot and examined it carefully, while April sat and watched him, feeling more miserable than she had ever done in her life before. 'Hmm,' he said, after a study of the inflamed ankle. 'Nasty!' He lowered it again and stood up. 'Still, it's soon remedied.'

So that, April thought ruefully, was all the sympathy she could expect, and she sat with tight-clenched hands while he'd gone, trying to be reasonable about it but unable to do more than allow for the fact that he could not have known that she would be allergic to the wretched liniment he had used.

What he put on it this time she did not question, for she recognized the clean, healthy smell of a well-known disinfectant which stung for only a few minutes before the irritation died down, and she supposed she should have been grateful for that much relief. Her self-pity, however, was still at a pitch and she could not bring herself to speak without, she was certain, bursting into tears again.

'Does that feel better?' She nodded, refusing to look at him. 'I didn't expect you to be allergic to the liniment,' he admitted. 'Although I suppose I might have guessed that if anything *could* go wrong it would, with your record for mishaps.'

She bit her lip in a last effort to keep back the tears. He was even blaming her for being allergic to that wretched stuff he had used, as she guessed he would. Two large, fat tears rolled down her cheeks at last and plopped on to her tightly clenched hands, and she heard him move on the settee beside her. Move to sit closer to her on the narrow seat.

'April!' A soothing hand brushed back her hair from her face, then lay against her neck, the fingers moving in a gentle, caressing gesture. 'Don't cry.'

'I – I can't help it.'

'It'll soon feel better. I promise.'

'That's – that's what you said about the – the liniment,' she accused, between the sobs that kept actual weeping at bay.

'So I did.' He cupped her face in his hand and pulled a rueful face, though she still refused to look at him. 'I'm sorry, April, but honestly I've never known it to have an adverse effect on anybody else.'

'It – it looks so horrible!' she declared and, as she had feared, started crying again in earnest. 'Oh! Oh, *damn* it – I didn't *want* to cry!'

'Aaah! Poor baby!' She glared up at him through her tears, then a second later buried her face against his chest, letting the tears flow freely, while he held her tight, one hand ruffling soothingly through her hair. 'You cry if it makes you feel better.'

'It – it doesn't.' Her voice was muffled, and she heard him laugh softly, hugging her closer for a moment, his face resting on the softness of her hair.

'Then don't, my sweet.'

The endearment, spoken in that warm, deep voice, sent a trickle of warning over her and she raised her head at last, leaning back against the cushions, as far away from him as she could get. She remembered Donald's inference than Nick's reputation was not exactly monastic, and she had no desire to become any deeper involved with him than she could help. Such a situation could lead to almost anything, and she lowered her eyes to shut out the humorous, mocking expression in his.

One dark brow lifted expressively and he looked down at her. '*Now* what have I said?' he asked.

'Nothing. Nothing at all,' she denied hastily. 'I'm – I'm sorry I was such a baby, Nick, but I feel much better now, thank you.'

'Good.' He still studied her with those curious, tip-tilted eyes that always seemed to be laughing at her. 'Any time you want a shoulder, just call.'

'I'll remember.'

He still sat facing her, and much too close for her peace of mind, studying her curiously, obviously puzzled by her manner. 'What's wrong, April?'

She would have given a great deal to be able to get up off the settee and walk out of the room, but she could not even move with him sitting there, waiting. 'Nothing's wrong,' she declared, as off-hand as she knew how, but he shook his head.

'Oh yes, it is,' he insisted. 'One minute you're quite content to sob out your woes in my arms and the next you're behaving like some virtuous little – well, you name it. I'd like to know what brought on the change.'

April curled her fingers into her palms, wishing yet again that she had not been so impulsive and allowed herself the luxury of weeping. 'I was *not* in your arms, as you call it,' she denied. 'I was upset and I cried, that's all. The rest was purely incidental, you just – just happened to be there.'

'Oh, I see.' She should have taken warning from the soft, quiet tone of his voice and the sudden bright glitter in his eyes, but his reaching out for her was so unexpected that she cried out in surprise before his mouth came down over hers and silenced her. 'Well, put that down as being purely incidental as well,' he told her, seconds later, and laughed softly as he walked out of the room.

CHAPTER FIVE

IT was not too long before April was about again on the injured ankle, and she returned to normality with relief. Sitting about all day was not suited to her temperament and she supposed that now she was able to get about normally she would be expected to return to the practice of helping Nick to exercise his horses. She was uncertain whether the idea of it pleased her or not, but she enjoyed the prospect of being mobile again, and at least she would be more so mounted on Dingo than she would on her own two feet.

'Do you feel like riding this morning?' Nick asked as they sat over breakfast, and she smiled at the coincidence. He noticed the smile and cocked a curious brow at her. 'Have I said something funny?' he asked.

'No.' She carefully spread butter on her toast and gave the job all her attention. 'It was just the – the coincidence that made me smile, that's all.'

'What coincidence?'

She took a bite out of her toast and made him wait while she ate it before she answered. 'The coincidence that made you ask me if I was riding this morning,' she said. 'You see, I was just thinking that any day now you'd be shanghaiing me into being your stable boy again.'

'Did you now?' He rested his elbows on the table and looked at her over the rim of his coffee cup. 'But I didn't exactly shanghai you into the job, did I?' he asked, and April laughed shortly.

'Hah! I'd like to know what else you'd call it,' she told him.

'A suggestion I thought was a good one?' he said, and

she shook her head.

'But you knew I didn't *want* to ride,' she objected. 'I told you so over and over again.'

'But you came.'

'I know I did eventually, because you left me with the impression that I'd be cut off without a penny if I didn't ride your blessed horses,' she retorted.

'And that was important to you, wasn't it?' he asked softly, and in such a way that April looked at him suspiciously.

'You know it isn't that important,' she told him. 'I have no objection to being rich – who has? But I was threatened with Uncle Simon's disapproval if I didn't do as you said.'

'Is that how it sounded?'

'It's how you meant it to sound, Nick.'

'I'm sure I didn't.' He sounded almost indignant, but it was pretty obvious he was laughing at her.

'Oh yes, you did. You told me Uncle Simon would expect me to earn my keep.'

'You think he does?'

'I – I don't know. He seemed pleased that I was going to help you, if you can call it helping, and I took your word for it that he would be displeased if I *didn't* do it.'

'I'm flattered you took my word for it.'

'I should have had more sense, I suppose,' April went on, recklessly. 'You must be used to talking women into doing what you want them to do.'

'Really?' The brown eyes watched her curiously now, although she thought he still found the situation well to his liking. 'Now where, sweet coz, did you get that outrageous idea from?' She did not answer and he sat for a moment sipping his coffee, his expression thoughtful and, she thought, slightly malicious. 'Could it have been Donald, I wonder?' he guessed softly, at last, and April flushed.

'No, it wasn't Do—'

'Liar!'

She looked up sharply and her eyes sparkled with anger at being attacked so unexpectedly. 'Don't you dare talk to me like that!' she told him indignantly. 'I'm not a little girl now, I'm entitled to a little respect.'

'Not when you listen to malicious gossip, you're not,' he retorted.

'Malicious?' She stuck out her chin. 'Or uncomfortably true? It's supposed to be fairly common knowledge, so I understand.'

'Is it?' He looked more interested than annoyed.

'Do you deny it?'

He laughed quietly and she had the uneasy feeling that she was about to get the worst of an argument, yet again. 'I don't have to deny it,' he told her, and regarded her quizzically, waiting for her next move, she thought wryly.

She looked at him a bit uncertainly. 'Because it's true?'

'Because it doesn't concern anyone else but me,' he said. 'Unless,' he added softly, 'you're personally interested?'

April felt the inevitable flush warm her cheeks and knew he was laughing at her. 'Of course I'm not,' she denied. 'I told you, I'm long over *that* childish infatuation.'

'Then I don't see that it concerns anyone else what I do with my own time,' he said. 'Do you?'

'In other words you're telling me I'm being too inquisitive. Is that it?'

He shook his head, laughing softly at the suggestion. 'Not exactly,' he demurred obligingly. 'You poke your pretty little nose in anywhere you like, but I'd be grateful if you'd ask your boy-friend not to hand on every bit of tittle-tattle he hears about me.' He swept her with that look that stirred her pulse and made her hastily lower her eyes. 'Actually,' he said slowly, 'I'd have thought he had plenty of *much* more interesting things to do when he was with you than discuss my affairs.'

'Donald's just a friend,' she informed him stiffly, feeling she had been firmly put in her place, however obliquely. 'A mutual friend, I might point out, *not* my boy-friend.'

His smile infuriated her with its complacency, and the accompanying apology she took as completely insincere. 'I'm sorry,' he said. 'Another case of misunderstanding. Do I gather I'm jumping the gun?'

April looked at him almost reproachfully, wishing she knew herself just how serious Donald was getting about her. So far he had behaved with quite formal restraint, except for that one time when he had spoken so freely. The evening he had taken her for a ride.

'You *are* jumping the gun,' she told him. 'There's — there's nothing like that between Donald and me; he always behaves perfectly.'

'How dull for you!'

Too late she saw the taunt for what it was, and his chuckle made her clench her hands into tight little fists on the table as she glared at him.

'I know you don't like Donald,' she said, 'but you don't have to be so — so condescending about him or me.'

'I *don't* dislike him,' he denied. 'I've always got on with Don.'

She looked at him suspiciously. 'It doesn't sound like it.'

'Well, I do,' he insisted, rather self-righteously, she felt. 'He's a sensible, hard-working chap, and good-looking too. None of which can be said about me,' he added.

His air of injured innocence was proving almost too

much for her self-control. 'I have to agree with you there,' she informed him, knowing that if she looked at him she would almost inevitably laugh.

'I thought you would.' He looked as hangdog as if his self-confidence rested on her opinion. 'We're like a pair of china dogs on a mantelpiece,' he added lugubriously. 'Me and Donald. Vice and Virtue.'

April could feel the laughter bubbling up inside her. 'Not quite as bad as that,' she denied. 'You do *have* good points, Nick.'

He reached across the table and took her hand in his, raising its palm to his lips. 'Appreciation,' he breathed ecstatically. 'Appreciation at last!'

It was too much for her. The exaggerated gesture, the pseudo-humility were so out of character that she laughed. More strictly speaking she giggled and was immediately reminded of her schoolgirl image as she looked at him. 'You *are* an idiot,' she said.

He still held her hands and raised her fingers to his lips. 'About some things,' he agreed softly, and held her gaze for a long moment before releasing her hand. 'Ah well.' He swallowed another mouthful of coffee and got to his feet. 'Are you taking out Dingo this morning for me?'

'If you want me to.'

'I do, please, I'm going to be rather busy with one thing and t'other.'

She nodded with her mouth full of toast. 'Mmm. I'll go and change as soon as I've finished breakfast.'

'You're sure you're up to it?'

She smiled and made a face at him. 'Such consideration!' she taunted. 'You're slipping, Nick.'

'And you're sassy,' he retorted. 'Get on with that toast while I go and saddle Dingo for you.'

She found her mount ready saddled and waiting for her as he had promised, when she went out to the yard, but there was no sign of Nick and she looked around her curiously. She was not yet sure enough either of her skill or her recently recovered ankle to like mounting unaided.

'Nick!' She waited, but there was no reply, and she frowned. 'Nick! Where are you?'

Only Dingo's restless feet stirred in the yard and the sound of the other animals in the paddock, made uneasy by the tone of her voice. 'Nick!' She went into the stable and saw that all the residents had been put into the paddock and only the dim, cool mustiness of silence greeted her, so that she frowned more deeply as she walked out into the bright sunshine again.

Wherever he was Nick was definitely not in the yard or the stable, and she began to wonder if he had perhaps got tired of waiting and gone without her. She had just noted that the bay he usually rode first thing was missing from the field, when Widgeon appeared.

He looked rather dim-witted, as he usually did, but April greeted him with a hopeful smile. 'Good morning,' she called. 'Have you seen Mr. Lawton about lately?'

The man nodded his nearly bald head. 'Saw him earlier, miss.'

'Earlier? You mean before he had breakfast?'

The head shook this time, and he took up a broom and started brushing out the nearest stall. 'Oh no, miss, about ten minutes since, that's all.'

April sighed, resignedly. 'And where is he now, do you know?'

'He went off, miss.' The broom did not pause in its labours and April nodded, as if her suspicions had been confirmed.

'I suppose he got tired of waiting for me,' she guessed, 'and went off alone.'

For a moment the balding head was raised and he looked at her with a sort of speculative craftiness. 'Oh no, miss, he weren't alone. Miss Graves was with him.'

'Oh! Oh, I see.' She stood there, horribly uncertain, sensing the man's curiosity, and she could not have said why she should suddenly feel rather hurt and let down. It would not have mattered so much if Nick had said he was riding with Fenella Graves. She looked at the man, still vigorously wielding his broom, and made up her mind. 'Will you give me a hand?' she asked.

She was helped into the saddle not nearly as efficiently as Nick would have done it, and she put cautious heels to the impatient Dingo. She was apparently expected to fulfil her role as groom whether alone or not, so she would do just that.

Dingo was restless from too long standing and took more holding than usual, but she dared not let him go any faster until she was sure of herself after the break from riding. It was surprising, she found, how easily it came back to her and before long she felt completely confident and made up her mind to enjoy her ride on her own.

It was lovely riding across the sunny meadow that sloped down to the stream where she had so disastrously come to grief. This time, she told herself, she was in complete control and she even dared to bring Dingo up to a trot as she neared the slope, remembering this time to sit back, even though she was preoccupied.

The stream looked cool and sparkling in the sun and she sent her mount splashing through it without pause, going, almost without realizing it, in the direction of Jordan's. She rode across the meadow on the other side and approached the farmhouse, a little diffidently since she was not sure if she would be welcome so early in the morning. Donald was a working farmer, despite his taste for fast and expensive cars, and he might not take kindly to visitors while he was busy. She was well over to the side of the meadow and if she was to call at Jordan's she would have to change course.

Dingo seemed to guess where she was going even before she decided to risk being unwelcome, and he signalled his intention of going that way almost before she had time to turn him. She was getting quite close to the gated yard when she suddenly lifted her head to better hear the voices that reached her on the wind.

Nick! She recognized the deep laugh and the voice and reined in her mount hastily. It appeared that Donald had other visitors this morning too, and ones she had no particular wish to encounter at this moment. The farm buildings made excellent cover and she took Dingo round as close as she could get behind them to avoid being seen.

It seemed an endless time before she heard the gate opened and Nick and Fenella Graves emerge, shouting their farewells to Donald, and she gave them ample time to get out of sight and earshot before she made her own way to the yard, feeling suddenly rather foolishly secretive as Donald came forward to meet her.

'April!' He looked pleasantly surprised, much to her relief, and he came over and helped her down. 'This is a wonderful surprise.'

'You're not too busy to bother with me?'

He shook his head firmly. 'Never!' he vowed. 'I'm delighted you came to see me.'

'Well, in truth,' she confessed, 'I just happened to come this way.' She laughed, slightly embarrassed, as he took her hand and led her into the house. 'I must confess that I didn't really set out to visit you, Donald.'

'Well, you're here anyway,' he said, 'and that's all that matters.' He glanced at her, suddenly curious. 'You only just missed Nick and Fenella, did you realize that?'

'I took good care to miss them,' April confessed ruefully. 'Fortunately I heard them and waited until they went before I put in an appearance.'

'Oh? Are you trying to avoid them for some reason or other?'

He took her into the small, cosy room she remembered from her last visit, and signed her to an armchair. 'In a way,' she agreed. 'I – well, I didn't want them to think I'd followed them from Kinley deliberately, it would have been much too embarrassing.'

'Would they have thought that?'

She made a wry face, wondering if she was right in her assumption. 'Nick would have, almost inevitably,' she told him. 'And Fenella – well, who knows what construction she'd put on it.'

'To be honest,' Donald said, 'I was rather surprised not to see you with them.'

'I – I rather thought I was riding with Nick this morning,' April told him, 'but when I got to the stable he'd already gone and Widgeon said he'd ridden off with Miss Graves, so—' She shrugged resignedly, trying to appear as if it bothered her not at all. 'I took it I'd been dismissed in favour of something more exciting.'

'He brought Fenella over to—'

April shook her head hastily. 'I don't want to talk about Nick and his fancies,' she told him lightly. 'Let's forget him, shall we?'

'I'm only too pleased to,' Donald obliged, but she could see that he was still curious and wished she had chosen to come anywhere but Jordan's this morning.

She looked around the room they were in, and smiled. 'I like this room, Donald, it's – homely.'

Donald smiled ruefully. 'It needs a woman's touch,' he told her, and she pulled a face.

'Isn't that just an old-fashioned fallacy?' she asked.

'I don't think so.' He seemed to be treating the subject seriously. 'I don't know what the difference is, but there is one. Something's missing somehow.'

'But you have a housekeeper.'

'A *daily* housekeeper,' he reminded her. 'It's not the same as having a woman around all the time.'

'You mean an unpaid full-time housekeeper, in other words a wife?' she laughed, and shook her head. 'There's only one answer to that, Donald.' She realized almost as soon as the words left her lips and she saw the quick, hopeful look that sprang into his eyes that she had perhaps been a little rash to say that.

'I've never thought about marrying until lately,' he confessed. 'Now I'm seriously thinking about it.'

'And giving up your freedom?' She tried to tease him, but he had neither Nick's talent for repartee nor his light-hearted view of life. 'I thought you were a confirmed bachelor like me.'

He leaned across from his own armchair close beside her and took her hand in his, his eyes wary and uncertain, but determined to press on, it seemed. 'I'm not a confirmed bachelor, April, not any more.'

She laughed and shook her head, feeling things getting a little out of hand. 'Then you'll have to be expelled from the bachelors' club,' she told him.

'April!' His fingers tightened their hold. 'April, you don't mean that do you? About being a confirmed bachelor girl?'

'Most certainly I do.'

He shook his head, looking down at their hands, clasped together. 'I hope you don't,' he said. 'At least I hope you're open to persuasion.'

It would be very unfair, she thought, to tease him the way she would have Nick, because he would take her so much more seriously and be so much more easily hurt. 'It — it would take a great deal of persuasion, Donald,' she told him. 'I have a lot to lose.'

She had spoken without thinking and was puzzled for a moment by his look of startled surprise. 'Oh yes, of course – the money.'

'Money?' She saw his meaning at last and felt her cheeks colour warmly. Everyone, she thought, seemed determined to attribute her with mercenary motives. 'Good heavens, no,' she told him. 'I was referring to my independence and my job. I wouldn't be willing to surrender those easily.'

'But you did it to come to Kinley,' he reminded her, and April sighed.

'Because Uncle Simon is a very old man and – well, in a way I'm quite fond of him. I suppose I always was, although he used to terrify me as a child. He wanted me to come to Kinley for a while, so I came. I suppose,' she allowed cautiously, 'the idea of one day being a wealthy woman was at the back of my mind, but I try not to think it was my main reason for coming here.'

'Oh, I'm sure it wasn't,' he assured her earnestly. 'But I'd hate to see you go away again, April.'

'Donald—'

'I mean it, sincerely.'

She smiled, looking at the serious, good-looking and thinking that perhaps she was really seeing h the first time in another light. Someone other than acquaintance who still felt a certain youthful her. He was no longer a boy of seventeen and s longer a schoolgirl; they were both mature, gent adults and both attractive enough for i sible that more than youthful nostalgia friendship going.

She put her free hand to his face, her e understanding. 'I know you mean it, D softly, 'and I'm very flattered.'

'This isn't a teenage crush, you kn

feel very deeply for you, April.'

'I – I know.'

'But you don't feel the same way about me, do you?' He sounded as if it was no more or less than he had expected and sighed, without giving her time to answer. 'Oh well, I refuse to give up hope. I'll just hope to win you round before you go off again to London.'

April left the farm to ride back to Kinley, feeling that her visit had been far more unsettling than she had expected. It seemed that Donald's feeling for her had changed little in the last seven years, only matured. He still considered himself in love with her, that was fairly obvious, although he had not said as much in so many words.

She rode back across the meadow and was nearing the stream when she heard her name called and turned, half-startled, to see Nick riding across from another direction towards her. He had evidently seen Fenella Graves safely home and was now prepared to spare a little time for her.

She felt a flash of resentment when she remembered the way she had looked for him to accompany her, before setting out, and some impulse made her put her heels to her mount instead of reining in to wait for him.

Dingo went tearing across the field at full gallop, and her attention was concentrated on staying in the saddle, realizing that she was riding for a possible fall, but caring at the moment.

She could hear Nick's horse thudding over the ground and her and urged Dingo on to greater efforts, determined not to be caught. If Nick had not wanted her company earlier, she could well do without his now. 'Come on, don't let them catch us,' she urged the all too willing horse, as the wind whipped her hair back from her

82

face and the speed stirred a strange kind of excitement in her. Let Nick catch her if he could, but she would give him a run for his money, however foolhardy he considered her. And she had no doubt what his opinion of her behaviour would be.

'April!' She heard his voice reach her faintly, but did not dare turn round to see how near he was. 'April!'

Dingo, by now, had caught her mood and he surged on through the stream, determined to leave his stable-mate behind, although he had little hope of outpacing the tall, long-legged bay that Nick rode.

'Slow down!' Nick's voice sounded closer now and she guessed that the bay too had been given his head. 'April!'

She crouched low over her mount's neck, feeling her arms and legs at last beginning to ache with the strain of holding him, and wondering how much longer she could go on and still control the enthusiastic Dingo. It was only seconds, however, before the bay came up alongside and Nick's right hand reached over for the rein.

His face, she could see when she chanced a hasty glance at him, was so grim that she scarcely recognized him. The wide mouth was set firm and the brows drawn down sternly together. She lent her weight to the rein almost automatically and the two animals gradually lost speed, each tossing his head, reluctant to end the chase.

Nick was out of the saddle in a second and came round to stand immediately below her, his eyes hard and blazing as he reached up and pulled her from her horse, his hands so tight around her waist that she put her own over them to try and ease the grip.

'You damned little idiot,' he snapped. 'What the devil do you think you're trying to do?'

He glared down at her darkly and, for once, April felt as if she had the upper hand. He was definitely shaken, though from fear for her rather than himself, she knew, while she still felt the thrill and excitement of the gallop and lifted her chin to look at him down the length of her small nose.

'We were giving you a run for your money,' she informed him.

'You could have broken your neck. Don't you realize that?' he demanded, and April laughed.

'Didn't you like the competition?' she taunted, and squealed a protest when he shook her.

'It was no competition,' he told her shortly. 'And if you ever do anything as foolhardy again, I'll—' He held her for a moment longer, his eyes dark with something she dared not try to interpret, but he was already beginning to relax and a moment later he shook his head and laughed. 'Just don't try to run before you can walk,' he said.

'I was doing all right,' April retorted, pushing his hands away from her waist. 'You just didn't like the fact that I was doing so well, *and* out-running you.'

'Out-running me?' He laughed and shook his head. 'Not on Dingo you wouldn't – he's fast, but he can't touch the bay when it comes to sheer speed. You weren't heading for anything other than a nasty fall,' he told her with a confident smile.

'Nonsense!'

'Nonsense nothing!' He eyed her for a moment and she could guess what was to come next even before he spoke. 'What came over you anyway? Why did you run off like that?'

April looked down at her hands, unwilling to give him the real reason for her impulsive, headlong flight. 'I just – I just didn't feel like company,' she said.

He cocked a brow at her. 'Any company, or just *my* company?' She did not reply and he put a hand under her chin and raised her face. 'Shall I guess?' he asked quietly, and did not wait for a reply. 'Was it because you knew I'd been over to Jordan's with Fenella?'

'It's of no consequence to me *where* you've been,' she informed him haughtily, and tightened her fists when he laughed.

'You thought you'd teach me a lesson, I suppose,' he went on, undeterred. 'Because Widgeon didn't give you the message I left with him, I should guess. Did he?' She shook her head and he sighed. 'Oh well, I should have had more sense than to leave it to him to tell you,' he said. 'But Fenella was in a hurry and I hate to keep a lady waiting.'

April looked at him reproachfully. 'I suppose I don't count as a lady, do I?'

He smiled, one hand touching her face gently. 'Oh yes, you do,' he said softly, 'but I thought you'd understand. Fenella's buying a horse from Don and she wanted my opinion. She came over at the last minute and asked me if I'd go with her.'

'Oh! Oh, I see.'

'Oh, you see,' he mocked gently. 'You see there was no need for you to risk breaking your beautiful neck just to show me that you disapproved of me going off with Fenella and leaving you.' She closed her eyes instinctively when he kissed her mouth briefly. 'I'm very flattered, however,' he added softly, 'that you were jealous enough to do it.' And April tried hard to find words to protest how wrong he was.

CHAPTER SIX

April rested her chin on her folded hands on top of the paddock fence and thought how peaceful everything seemed. It was growing quite late in summer and she had acquired a tan she was rather proud of during the weeks she had been at Kinley. She never tanned very darkly, but the golden-skinned look did wonders for her blue eyes.

During the daytime she spent a good deal of time with Nick and rather more with Donald in the evenings. He came for her in either one or the other of his cars, ready and willing to demonstrate his prowess as a driver. Nick, she thought, found this extrovert streak in an otherwise reserved character, rather amusing. But then Nick found a good many things amusing, not least of all April herself.

She had only once seen him get anywhere near to losing his temper and that was when she had deliberately sent her horse galloping up the slope from Jordan's to escape him. A feat she had never yet repeated.

She leaned on the paddock fence beside Nick, watching the graceful antics of the two long-legged foals. One of them, April's favourite, was a pretty creature with a dark brown coat and a white blaze in the shape of a star on his forehead. She had christened him Starlight almost the first time she saw him, and the name had stuck.

'Do you remember going to Pickett Fair?' Nick asked suddenly, and she frowned for a moment, trying to remember.

'I have a vague recollection of going to some sort of a fair when I was here before,' she told him.

'I took you and Aunt Betty.'

'Yes, yes, I do remember.'

'How would you like to go again?'

'Very much,' April said unhesitatingly, and looked at him from under her lashes, smiling. 'Why? Are you offering to take me again?'

He laughed, resting one foot on the fence and propping an elbow on it. 'I might take you again if you're very good.'

April pulled a face at him. 'How good is very good?'

'Good enough,' he replied, and laughed. 'Always providing Don hasn't already asked you, of course,' he added, knowing full well that Donald had done no such thing.

April frowned at him. 'He hasn't,' she said. 'Is he likely to?'

He shrugged, his eyes quizzical. 'Quite likely to, I should say,' he told her. 'He goes most years and I'll be very surprised if he doesn't ask you to go with him this time.'

She rested her chin on her hands and gazed at the peaceful meadow, uncertain if she quite followed his reasoning. Nick could be very enigmatic sometimes. 'Is that why you asked me to go with you?' she asked, and he laughed.

'As a matter of fact it isn't,' he said. 'I never gave Don a thought until after I'd spoken, and it's obvious you hadn't either.' He cocked a brow at her, his smile too knowing by far for her liking. 'Now I suppose you'll want to change your mind,' he suggested.

'No, I shan't.'

She sounded very sure about it, but she wondered how she would feel when and if Donald did ask her to go with him. He could be very touchy on the subject of Nick, as she had already discovered. It was a little puzzling, too, why Nick had not asked Fenella Graves to go with him, unless fairs were not her taste.

Nick smiled wryly. 'I think I'll wait and see how you feel when Don actually asks you,' he said. 'And see if you're as enthusiastic then.'

'You have a pretty poor opinion of me if you think I chop and change as the mood takes me,' she objected. 'I'm quite happy to go with you whether Donald asks me or not, and he – he may not even ask me.'

'Oh, he will.' A wide grin foresaw future difficulties with little worry, apparently. 'He's still moon-eyed over you.'

April turned her head and frowned at him. 'That's ridiculous, Nick,' she argued. 'He's *not* moon-eyed over me, that's – that's schoolboy talk. He – he likes me, that's all.'

'*Likes* you?' His eyes teased her unmercifully. 'He'd swim from here to China for you, and you know it.'

'That's nonsense!'

'Is it?'

'Yes, it is,' April insisted. She remembered suddenly Donald's assertion that day at the farm when he had told her how deep his feeling was for her, but she refused to let Nick know about that and she was certainly not prepared to be teased about it. 'You've no right to make such personal observations, either. It's – it's outrageous.'

'Outrageous?' He laughed delightedly. 'What a lovely, Victorian-sounding word that is! You do exaggerate, April.'

'I'm not exaggerating!'

'I'd go so far as to say he's in love with you,' he insisted, 'and I'm *not* exaggerating.'

'You are, and I wish you'd keep out of my affairs, Nick.'

'Affairs?' He raised a scandalized brow and she felt the colour in her cheeks.

'You know quite well what I mean.'

'I do, dear girl, but it did sound rather exciting for a moment. I began to think that Don and I were just two in a long line of lovers.'

'Oh, you—'

His laugh cut her short and she was obliged to respond to it with a half-rueful smile. 'I suppose it did sound a bit – a bit off,' she allowed. 'But sometimes you can be the most maddening man, Nick, and I could quite easily hate the sight of you.'

'Aaah, could you?' His eyes mocked her seriousness. 'Aren't you coming to the fair with me after all?'

April lifted her chin and looked at him down the length of her nose. 'Yes, I am, even if it's just to teach you a lesson. Unless,' she added with a swift glance from under her lashes, 'you've had second thoughts. If you want to take someone else, for instance.'

He met her gaze and his own was as steady and amused as ever. 'Who else, for instance?'

'Fenella?'

He shook his head slowly. 'No,' he said, 'there's no one else I'd rather take.' She held his gaze for a moment, then hastily lowered her own, her pulse tapping away busily at her temple as she rested her chin on her hands again.

They were silent for several minutes, the stillness of the August evening scarcely broken by the quiet stirrings of the horses in the paddock and the sound of the birds returning to the rookery in the trees at the edge of the meadow. All evenings should be as peaceful as this, April thought, and closed her eyes on the sheer pleasure of it.

'What do we do at this fair?' she asked, after a while, and Nick turned his head lazily and smiled.

'It depends,' he said, 'what you want to do.'

'Is it an ordinary fair with roundabouts and things?'

He nodded. 'In part,' he agreed. 'But it's also the annual horse-fair.'

'Oh!' She instinctively looked across to where Starlight and his mother cropped the short grass lazily and as if he sensed something in her voice, he cocked a curious brow at her.

'Don't you like the idea of that?' he asked.

April shook her head. 'Not very much,' she admitted, wondering if he would laugh at her. 'I – I always feel rather sorry for the animals.' She looked again at Starlight, her eyes betraying her own private little worry. 'You're not—'

He shook his head smiling, but at least not laughing at her. 'Don't worry, Starlight is safe – at least for another year.'

'I hate to think of him being sold at all,' April said. 'I know it's silly and he has to be some time or other, but he's so adorable.'

'And you think I'm terribly hard-hearted for even thinking about selling him?'

'I didn't say that, Nick. After all, I – I suppose it's your business, isn't it?'

'A business you don't altogether approve of?' She did not reply and he shook his head, half-smiling. 'It's not only me who trades in horses,' he told her. 'As a matter of fact I bought Penny, Starlight's mother, from Don.'

It was one way of reminding her, April thought, that Donald too traded in horses and should therefore come in for his share of her disapproval, and she smiled to think of him being so vulnerable as to care either way.

'I don't consider Donald any more of a – a saint than you are,' she told him, and Nick laughed.

'I'm glad to hear it, although I'm sure if Don knew how much you disapproved he'd stop right away rather than risk incurring your displeasure.'

April flushed, unwilling to return to the subject of Donald. 'Donald's a business man just as you are,' she told him shortly. 'He'd do no such thing.'

Nick shook his head, his serious expression belied by the wicked glint in his eyes as he regarded her pink cheeks. 'Ah, but he *is* in love,' he said, 'and it shows.'

'Must you?' April retorted. 'We've already disposed of the subject of Donald. We're both sensible adults now and he got over me in the same way I shed my youthful crush on you.'

She had worded it like that deliberately to provoke him. 'You may have shed me, angel,' he said softly, 'but Don's made of sterner stuff. He's a stayer.' His eyes mocked her, their tip-tilted corners crinkled when he laughed. 'You might as well face it.'

She sought for words for a moment, then gave up and glared at him despairingly. 'Oh! Oh, for heaven's sake, Nick, let's change the subject!'

He was still laughing, his chin resting on one hand his elbow on the fence, all his attention centred on her. 'If you like,' he agreed magnanimously.

'I—' She saw Fenella Graves at that moment, coming through the gate from the garden. 'You have company,' she told him, and he turned lazily.

Nick's welcome could have been said to lack warmth, but Fenella appeared not to notice and she smiled brightly as she came towards them, looking sleek and sophisticated and completely out of place in the stable yard.

'Nick darling!' She beamed her pleasure at seeing him, acknowledging April with a brief nod, a gesture that April returned without attempting to enlarge on it, for she had been snubbed too often already to risk another.

'Hello, Fen.' He smiled at her inquiringly. 'What brings you to Kinley?'

'Why you, darling, of course.'

'Of course,' he mocked, and she laughed.

Fenella's blonde head was neat and tidy, not a hair out

of place, and her make-up was impeccable, so that April, with her windblown hair and her make-up consisting of no more than a trace of lipstick, felt terribly gauche and schoolgirlish suddenly. She was wearing a simple cotton dress too, while Fenella was band-box smart in some cream-coloured creation that looked wildly expensive.

Fenella thrust a possessive arm through Nick's, the fingers curled tightly, and she smiled up at him. 'Darling, I was on my way home and I suddenly thought that this was a marvellous opportunity to see your new arrivals.'

'Well – there they are.' He waved a casual hand at the two foals and their mothers, and Fenella made suitable cooing noises, her smile unnaturally benign.

'Oh, Nick, they're *sweet*! They're utterly sweet.'

'They're a healthy pair,' Nick agreed laconically.

'I adore that little one with the blaze,' Fenella enthused. 'He's a darling.'

Nick smiled. 'You mean Starlight,' he said. 'He seems to be general favourite. April makes a terrific fuss of him.'

'Starlight?' Fenella repeated the name. 'Oh, it's perfect, Nick, how clever of you.'

'Not me,' Nick informed her blandly. 'It was April's idea.'

'Oh. Oh, was it?' She considered the information for a moment, then smiled up at him in a way that was unmistakably coaxing. 'Whatever his name is, darling, I must have him.'

'Must you?'

April looked at Nick anxiously. Sooner or later, she supposed the colt would have to go. Someone would have him, but she hated the thought of it being Fenella Graves. It was silly of her, she supposed, but she had developed an almost possessive feeling for the little animal and hated the thought of parting with him.

'Well, it *is* my birthday next month,' Fenella coaxed. 'And I'm sure Daddy would buy him for me.'

'I'm sure he would,' Nick agreed, catching April's eye and smiling – a secret sort of smile that both puzzled and disturbed her. 'But Starlight's not for sale, Fen.'

'Not for—' She stared at him for a second as if she could not believe her ears, then she laughed, a harsh, throaty sound, and snuggled up to his arm, her glance reproachful. 'Oh, I see! Well, I won't say no to him as a present from *you*, darling.'

And that, April thought despairingly, was exactly what she had expected he would say. It was what she had been hinting at when she first spoke of having the colt. It was what Nick had meant when he gave April that secret smile. He intended giving Fenella the colt for a birthday present and April had been admitted to the secret.

But Nick was shaking his head and it took April a minute or two to realize it. 'I'm sorry, Fen,' he told her. 'I'm afraid you misunderstood me. I can't give Starlight to you because he isn't mine to give – he's April's.'

It would have been hard to tell who was most surprised by the statement, April or Fenella. They both stared at him for a moment, and April thanked heaven that the other woman had her back to her, at least until she could bring her obvious surprise under control.

There was silence for a long moment – a chill, brittle silence that April found distinctly disturbing, although Nick seemed quite unconcerned about the stir he had caused. It took a moment or two to dawn on her and then April looked across at the colt and felt a swift and sudden lilt of excitement. She resisted the impulse that urged her to throw her arms round his neck and kiss Nick resoundingly for his gift, not even stopping to think what crazy impulse had prompted him to make it.

Fenella's sharp hazel eyes turned to April at last and

noted her flushed cheeks and the unconcealable shine in her eyes, then a mockery of a smile touched the tight mouth. 'Congratulations,' she said acidly.

'I—' April began, unsure what she should say for the best. Almost certainly Fenella would take losing the colt to her as a personal affront and, April thought, she would not forget it easily.

It was Nick who came to her rescue. 'It's a sort of unbirthday present,' he explained blandly. 'April's very useful to me, you know.'

'Really?' An elegant back was again presented to April.

'Acting unpaid, of course,' Nick went on, either oblivious or uncaring. 'Starlight's by way of being a thankyou.'

'I see.' The cool voice was razor-edged. 'What do *I* have to do to be so generously thanked, Nick?'

He laughed, as if he found her venom as amusing as he did everything else. 'I don't need another stable-girl, thank you,' he told her. 'One's as many as I can handle.'

'At this rate,' Fenella retorted, 'I should think one is as many as you can afford.'

Simon Carver had shown little surprise when April told him that Nick had given her the colt. At least, she had qualified, she thought he had meant the gift seriously and not done it simply to avoid giving it to Fenella. She had had no opportunity to ask him about it yet.

'Well, why shouldn't he give the colt to you if he wants to?' he asked.

'For one thing,' April said, hoping it had been a genuine gift, 'he must be worth quite a bit of money. He's a beautiful little creature.'

The old man shrugged his thin shoulders. 'Nick doesn't

94

have to study the pennies to that extent,' he told her. 'It's only because he's too damned fond of his independence that he does anything at all.' It was obvious from the way he spoke that it was a trait he admired in his stepson, and April smiled.

'You know you like him the better for it, Uncle Simon,' she said. 'He told me you'd think more of me if I earned my keep, as he put it.'

'He told you that?' The weak blue eyes looked at her shrewdly. 'Is that why you help him with the horses?'

April nodded, pulling a wry face. 'In a way,' she admitted. 'I was more or less shanghaied into it.'

'Hmm. He's will of his own, that lad,' he told her, not without pride. 'Always did have.' He looked up as his stepson joined them. 'I hear you've given April the dark colt,' he said, and Nick smiled as he sat down.

'I have,' he admitted shortly.

'You were serious about it, then?'

Nicked looked up curiously at April. 'Of course I was,' he said. 'Didn't you think I was?'

'I – I wasn't sure.'

'I see.' His tip-tilted eyes crinkled into a smile. 'Is that why you haven't thanked me for it yet?'

'I'm sorry, Nick.' She looked down at her folded hands for a second, remembering that impulse that she had known when she first knew she had the colt, and she got to her feet, a small smile on her face as she stood looking down at him. 'Thank you, very, very much,' she said softly, 'I love him, Nick, I really do.'

She had intended only to kiss him lightly on his forehead, but as she bent over him he put his hands to her waist and pulled her down across his knees, his mouth silencing the beginnings of a protest. '*That's* more like it,' he said, when he released her, and she sat for a second or two on his lap, her cheeks burning and her eyes flicking uncertainly to her great-uncle.

She heard the harsh, low sound of the old man's chuckle, with disbelief, then she got to her feet again hastily and stood for a while with her back to the pair of them, looking out of the window. 'I – I wish you wouldn't do that, Nick,' she said, a little breathlessly, wishing too that her voice would not tremble the way it did.

'I thought you were doing it,' he declared. 'You *were* going to kiss me, weren't you?'

'Not – not like that,' she objected. 'But – I'm grateful to you for giving me Starlight. He's beautiful and I adore him, but—' She turned round and looked at him. 'He must be quite valuable, Nick. Are you sure you want to give him to me?'

'Quite sure.'

She stood by the window for a while longer, thinking of Starlight and the fact that she owned him. He was hers for as long as she wanted him, and now she would never have to see him sold to anyone. She smiled slowly at Nick. 'Thank you, Nick,' she said softly, at last, and sought to dismiss the persistent shadow of Fenella Graves.

It was only the following day that Donald spoke to her about going to the fair with him and, as she had expected, April felt rather mean when she was obliged to refuse.

'Don't you like fairs?' he asked without giving her time to explain her reason for refusing.

'I do,' April said, 'but – well, Nick's already asked me to go with him, Donald, and I said I would.'

Donald frowned. They were driving through the village and she wondered if it was a good idea to discuss anything as controversial as Nick while he was driving. 'I might have known,' he declared shortly.

'I'm sorry.'

'Oh, it's my own fault, I suppose,' he admitted, and

pulled a wry face at her over his shoulder. 'I just never anticipate Nick fast enough. Besides,' he added, 'I quite expected he'd take Fenella this year.'

April looked at him curiously, her own thoughts on that point re-aroused. 'Does he usually take Fenella?' she asked.

'When she's around, yes.'

'And this year she's around?'

'Yes. That's two of us he's disappointed.'

April pursed her lips thoughtfully. 'You could take her,' she suggested, and he laughed shortly.

'I could,' he agreed, 'but I won't. Fenella's not my cup of tea at all.'

April smiled ruefully, remembering his refusal to give her the colt she wanted. 'I'm not sure she's Nick's either,' she said.

'Oh?' She explained the incident of last evening, and Fenella's eventual disappointment, and she thought he was almost as displeased with the idea as Fenella had been. 'Why should he do that?' he asked. 'Did you ask him for the colt?'

'No, of course not, but he knows I love Starlight and he said it was a – a sort of thank-you.'

'Very generous of him.' He had his foot down hard on the accelerator and they were travelling even faster than April liked, for all her love of speed, although the road was fairly straight and wide, with very little traffic.

'He appreciates my helping with the horses,' she said, one hand holding on tight to the car door.

Donald laughed shortly. 'Considering he forced you into it, I should hope he would be grateful,' he told her. 'I suppose he was trying to square himself by giving you the colt.'

'Perhaps,' April agreed uneasily. 'Although I don't really mind helping out, you know, Donald. In fact I quite enjoy it.'

'Oh, I beg your pardon!' The sarcasm made her flush, and she would have made some sort of protest, except that at that moment they came to a bend in the road.

They were going much too fast and April thought he would not normally have been quite so foolhardy as not to reduce speed as they went into the bend, but he was angry about her going with Nick to the fair and about her admitting to her liking for the stable work she did, and he was less careful than usual.

They were half-way round the corner when she realized that there was another car coming towards them and she felt the wild, urgent hammering of her heart against her ribs when she knew with horrible certainty that a collision of some sort was inevitable.

Fortunately Donald's reactions were both more swift and more knowledgeable and he hastily swung the wheel over, missing the oncoming car by a fraction of an inch, and colliding instead with the thick resilience of a hedge. April hid her face, shaken but unhurt, and sat quite still for a second in the ensuing silence.

The other car too had stopped, and she raised her head in time to recognize Nick's face, dark with anger, his long legs striding swiftly and vengefully towards them. He came to April first and looked down at her pale face and wide eyes, a kind of desperation in the look as if he could scarcely believe she was unhurt.

'Are you all right, April?' he asked, and she nodded without speaking. Hard fingers closed over her hand still clinging to the door and he bent closer to look into her face. 'Are you sure?'

'Yes. Yes, I'm O.K., Nick, really.'

'Hmm.' He scanned her face again, then glared angrily across at Donald, who looked almost as shaken as she did. 'What the hell are you trying to do?' he demanded, in a

98

voice that April scarcely recognized. 'You were doing a good eighty round that bend. Have you gone off your head?'

'I wasn't concentrating.' Donald swallowed hard on his injured pride, and April could not help feeling sorry for him. Nick, angry, was enough to overawe anyone, and especially someone in the wrong.

'At eighty miles an hour?' He glowered at Donald, who was recovering enough to resent it.

'No one's hurt, are they?' he asked sharply. 'And you were doing a pretty good speed yourself.'

'I was doing sixty,' Nick stated in a tone that was conviction enough for anybody. 'And I hadn't got a passenger.'

For the first time Donald looked at April, anxious to be reassured. 'April! Are you all right?'

She nodded. 'Quite O.K., Donald, thanks. Just a – a bit shaken.'

'You're lucky you weren't killed,' Nick informed her with brutal frankness.

'Now look here!' Donald's fair brows were gathered into a frown nearly as black as Nick's. 'I'm used to driving around these roads at high speeds, there's no question of anyone being killed.'

'High speeds are all right when you've got your mind on the job,' Nick told him shortly. 'In my opinion when you've a distracting passenger you should slow down. You should have enough sense to know that.'

'I don't give a damn for your opinion,' Donald retorted. 'Now get out of my way.'

'And I don't give a damn if you break your own blasted neck,' Nick informed him callously, 'but when you're driving with April you take care or I'll break it for you!'

It was obvious to April that continuing the argument

would only result in Donald losing it and it looked as if he must have shared her view, for he restarted the engine and put the car into reverse.

'Jordan!'

Donald reversed the car, and looked back. 'Please, Nick!' April too looked at the dark, vengeful figure in the shadow of the hedge, and her eyes pleaded for a truce.

For a moment Nick looked at her, his dark, tip-tilted eyes glowing with something that disturbed her deeply, then he waved an almost casual hand in dismissal and April could have sworn that, as they drove off, Donald heaved a sigh of relief.

She had expected some comment when she returned home after the eventful ride, but Nick appeared to have completely recovered his customary good humour, and she thanked heaven for it.

Her great-uncle had gone to his bed, and April and Nick sat at opposite ends of the sitting-room, April with a book which she was not really reading, and Nick poring over some accounts which seemed to be giving him some trouble. She had glanced up at him once or twice from under her lashes and seen that he was engrossed, but then he suddenly put down his pencil and cocked a quizzical brow at her.

'Is something bothering you?' he asked.

'Bothering me?' She gazed at him wide-eyed, uncertain, now that she had his attention, just why she had been watching him so surreptitiously.

He nodded. 'You've been watching me with what I can only describe a meaningful look,' he informed her. 'As if you expected something to happen.'

She hastily lowered her eyes. 'That's silly,' she declared. 'What makes you say that?'

'Maybe a sound knowledge of what makes females

tick,' he said with a smile that incited disagreement, and leaned back in his chair, looking at her speculatively. 'You're expecting me to say something about something,' he decided rather confoundingly. 'And I haven't so far come up to expectations. Am I right?'

'No, you're not,' April declared, but he laughed, obviously disbelieving.

'Have you recovered from your shaking up this morning?' he asked then, and she sat for a moment wondering how on earth he could have known what was in her mind when she hadn't even known herself until now.

'Yes – yes, thank you.'

'Good. I've never known Don crash one of his precious cars before. You must have proved quite a distraction.'

'He was terribly upset that it happened,' she told him, remembering the furious way he had berated Donald for risking her neck as well as his own.

'I expect he was,' he said airily. 'He could have killed the pair of you, not to mention me.'

'Oh, so that was it.' She put down her book, and got up from her chair, turning her back on him to look out of the window at the old moon sitting fatly in the sky. 'It was your own skin you were so concerned for when you lost your temper with Donald?'

She could not have explained what possessed her to make such a provocative statement when she knew quite well why he had been so angry with Donald, and she could almost feel the ensuing silence. Her heart was thudding against her ribs and the heavy pulse at her temple drummed wildly as she watched his dark reflection loom behind her, tall and somehow menacing in the yellow-lit room reflected in the window.

'That's right,' he said quietly, just behind her. 'Let him break *your* beautiful neck if he wants to – *I* don't care.'

Meeting his eyes in the shiny glass reflection gave her a

curious feeling of unreality, and she knew she was smiling only because she could see herself in the dark mirror – a small provocative smile she did not recognize as her own.

'I believe you,' she said, and laughed.

It was like every romantic moment she had conjured up as a fifteen-year-old when he kissed her, and her legs felt so weak they must surely have folded under her if he had not held her so tightly. Her hands slid round his rough, dark head and she felt as if she was slipping into some warm, exciting but perilous dream. Only when he released her mouth and buried his face in the soft dishevelment of her hair did she begin to come to her senses.

Standing there she could feel the strength and excitement that had always been Nick, but she knew she had long since outgrown Nick's particular brand of magic. A brand of magic he practised widely, if Donald was to be believed.

'Nick!'

He let her go with flattering reluctance, but watched her more curiously than reproachfully, his mouth crooked into a faint, almost derisory smile. 'Don't tell me you're shocked,' he said, 'because I shan't believe you, April.'

'Not – not shocked,' she allowed. 'I'm not so two-faced as to pretend that, but—'

'But?' he echoed softly, and April shook her head, picking up her abandoned book and hugging it to her as if for protection.

'I – I don't like promiscuity, Nick.'

'Promiscuity?' He repeated the word with some relish. 'Who? You or me?'

She flushed, embarrassment making her angry. As much with herself as with him, she freely admitted. 'I'd scarcely term my friendship with Donald as promiscuity,' she told him, and he laughed softly.

'But you'd term me anything that Donald cares to call it, eh?'

'I – I didn't say that. It's just that – well, you didn't really deny that you—' She hastily avoided the expression she saw in his eyes and shook her head, despairing of making any sense. 'I've no wish to be part of a harem,' she told him stiffly, and left the room as quickly as she could, slamming the door on the deep, derisive sound of his laughter.

rose to her feet. "I see. In that case I'm sorry I bothered you unnecessarily. I'll let you get on with your breakfast in

CHAPTER SEVEN

ALTHOUGH she was not very enthusiastic about the horse-fair, April was quite excited about visiting Pickett Fair with Nick and she looked forward to her day out. Since the best forgotten moment when he had kissed her so disturbingly they seemed to have compromised on a relationship that was not quite brother and sisterly, nor yet anything more romantic. Although she had the uneasy feeling that Nick would have quite happily let it drift towards the latter with very little encouragement.

She had taken his advice and dressed for their outing in comfortable sandals and a cool cotton dress, for August was, at the moment, as hot as July had been. She had had a momentary twinge of conscience about Donald, but had soon dismissed it as pointless. Donald could have asked her as soon or sooner than Nick had, but he had left it until it was too late.

There was noise and music from the fun-fair and April hoped that Nick's plans for them included at least a short whirl on the many traditional amusements. She had not visited a fun-fair for a good many years and she was in the mood to indulge her more bizarre instincts today.

She wrinkled her nose at the unmistakable smell of the crowded sale ring and pouted reproach at Nick when he laughed at her. 'You go and buy your horses,' she suggested, 'and I'll wander off and have a look at the fun fair until you've finished.'

'You'll do no such thing.' His hold on her arm tightened at the suggestion and she looked up, rather startled by his reaction.

'But I'll be perfectly O.K.,' she assured him. 'I won't get myself lost, I promise.'

'I know you won't,' Nick declared firmly, 'because I'm not letting you out of my sight. There're some pretty rough customers at these do's,' he added, 'and you're much too pretty to let loose in a crowd of doubtful characters.'

'But they're only farmers and – and country people,' she objected, but was nevertheless stirred by some inner excitement at his possessive attitude.

'And others,' he insisted. 'You stay close to me, my girl, or some roving-eyed diddicoy will be running off with you.'

April giggled, catching the eye of one such character even as he spoke. 'I've never been stolen by gypsies,' she told him. 'It might be quite fun.'

'Behave yourself!' The hand that held her arm shook her suddenly, and she looked up to meet a look that was both speculative and amused. 'I felt more sure of you when you were fifteen,' he told her.

'You had more reason to,' April retorted, her eyes dancing. 'I'd have been too scared to leave you then.'

'Well, be scared now,' he told her sternly, 'because you'll have every reason to be if you sneak off while I'm busy.'

She found herself quite fascinated, despite her former convictions, once the sale started, and got almost excited when Nick bid determinedly for a pretty little bay mare he had set his heart on. The animal was of good stock and her name, it appeared, was April Girl, so that it became more than ever a challenge to get her.

Nick was successful at last and he led the mare to the waiting horsebox, followed by a delighted April, who watched anxiously while she was loaded and driven off by Widgeon. 'She's lovely,' April enthused, enchanted by her namesake, and Nick laughed.

'Someone else thought so too,' he said. 'It was Fen Graves' man who gave me such a run for my money.'

April pulled a face. 'Oh dear! Fenella won't like that, will she?'

Nick looked around them at the milling crowd of people and raised a brow suddenly. 'I can see Fen over by the ring,' he told her. 'I'd better go and have a pacifying word with her, I think.'

'But—'

'You stay here where I can find you again,' Nick told her. 'I'll only be a second.'

April watched him go, her mouth downturned in reproach. So much for his being afraid of letting her go off on her own, she thought. He went off and left her to her own devices soon enough when Fenella Graves came along. It would serve him right if she took matters into her own hands and went to the fun-fair on her own.

After five minutes waiting for him to return, she was beginning to get angry with him for abandoning her so casually. A few minutes more and she was ready to explode. She had just made up her mind to walk off when a tentative hand touched her elbow and she turned sharply, remembering Nick's reference to rough characters.

A small, dark, monkey-like face peered at her from below a frizzle of grey hair, the rest of which was hidden by a faded red scarf knotted in traditional fashion on the nape of a scrawny neck. 'All alone, dearie?' The voice was thin and harsh and the smile completely toothless.

'I – not really,' April told her. 'I'm waiting for someone to come back.'

'Tell your fortune while you waits,' the crone offered, and leered persuasively. 'Come on, dearie, learn what's in store for you. You got a lucky face.'

Even as she shook her head, April was tempted. There was always a certain fascination about genuine gypsies, and she was certain that this old woman was the genuine article. 'No. No, thank you,' she said, and smiled to show that the refusal was without prejudice.

'Only take a minute, dear.' A thin hand was already reaching for hers, and she reluctantly allowed herself to be led aside, to where there was room to sit on some baled hay.

April glanced round uneasily, convinced that if Nick was to see her having her fortune told he would laugh at her gullibility. There was still no sign of him, however, and she resigned herself to waiting for him and to the old woman's ministrations.

The rheumy old eyes peered short-sightedly at her hands for several seconds, then she nodded her head slowly. 'You've had a sad life, dearie,' she was told. 'These near and dear was took early, but you've been lucky too.' She gave her attention to April's left hand, and nodded wisely over what it revealed. 'You'm goin' to be luckier still, my dear. Lots of money's comin' your way, though it means more sadness first. Another loss of someone close. But there's luck, dearie, lots of luck, and there's – there's *two* men I see.' A rasping chuckle delighted in the fact. 'A bonny girl like you 'as no call to go short of men. One's dark an' one's lighter.'

April blinked uneasily. Such accuracy could hardly be coincidental. And the mention of her parents' early deaths and the reference to Uncle Simon's money. It was nothing short of uncanny. 'Please – please go on,' she urged, unsure now much more she wanted to hear.

The crone pored over her hand again. 'You wants to know which one 'tis to be, don't you, my lovely?'

'I – yes, I suppose I do.'

The older woman held her hand, peering closely at the

lines criss-crossing her palm, but before she could speak a shadow fell across them both and they looked up, startled. It was the old gypsy who recovered her wits first, and she cackled knowingly as she greeted the newcomer.

'Oh, 'tis you, me handsome,' she said, and Nick laughed.

'Yes, it's me, you old rogue.' He looked at April, her cheeks pink with the embarrassment of being caught. 'What have you been telling my cousin, Bess?'

'Your cousin?' The small, shrewd eyes looked from one to the other. ' 'Tisn't that close, dearie, is it?' she asked.

Nick laughed, taking April's hand and pulling her to her feet. 'Not quite,' he admitted. 'I should have known better than to try to fool you, shouldn't I?'

The old woman nodded, her toothless grin wider than ever. 'That you should,' she told him. 'I told the lady's fortune, though, and 'tis only right I should be paid for it.'

'Of course.'

April saw the silver coin that changed hands and heard the old woman's satisfied chuckle as her fingers closed on it. 'Bless you, my dear, bless you.' She reached out and touched April's arm, her eyes narrowed and sharp. 'You watch out for the fair ones, dearie, they'm unlucky for you.'

'I – I will,' April promised, still in something of a daze and completely forgetting for the moment that she was angry with Nick for leaving her so long. She walked with her hand in Nick's and had a sudden clear picture of Fenella Graves' sleek blonde head while a shiver flicked like an icy finger down her spine.

'I never realized you had such odd friends,' she told Nick after a few minutes.

He looked at her and smiled slowly, a hint of mystery in his expression that reminded her of the old woman.

'Oh, I see old Bess every year at the fair,' he said. 'She's a regular visitor.'

'Is she a *real* gypsy?'

He nodded. 'The genuine article,' he assured her.

'She seemed to know an awful lot about me,' April said thoughtfully. 'All sorts of things about my past that she couldn't possibly have guessed.'

'Your past?' He arched a curious brow. 'Have you a past?'

'Of course I have,' April retorted. 'I mean she knew that my parents died when I was a baby, and she knew that I would – well, that I'll be coming into money one day. It was all a bit creepy really.'

'Is that all she told you?' he asked, and she thought he sounded quite seriously interested, which was not the kind of reaction she expected from Nick at all.

'Yes. It was all she had time to tell me before you came along.'

His laugh mocked her, but she still had the feeling that he was quite serious about his questions. 'Nothing about your love life?' he asked, and April flicked him a curious look.

'Not really,' she said. 'There wasn't time.' They said nothing for a while but walked, rather aimlessly, towards the fun-fair with its noise and excitement. 'Has she ever told you?' she asked suddenly, and thought that the hand holding hers tightened very briefly before he answered.

'Told my fortune, you mean? Yes, as a matter of fact, she has.'

'Did you – did you believe her?'

He was silent for a moment, then he looked down at her with something she would have sworn was sadness in his strange and unusual eyes. 'Yes, I think I did,' he told her quietly. 'You see, just three weeks before my mother died, Pop and I were visiting this fair and old Bess insisted on telling his fortune. We'd never seen her before that day, but I've never forgotten her since.'

'What – what did she tell you?' She was almost afraid to ask.

'It was what she told Pop. She said that he would lose someone close within a month, then she shut up like a clam and refused to say any more. They don't like telling bad news, you know.'

'Oh, Nick, that's – that's awful!'

'It upset Pop when he remembered it,' Nick told her. 'And he's never been to the fair since.'

'That must be a long time ago.'

'Fifteen years,' he said precisely, then shrugged off his new, uncharacteristic seriousness with a laugh. 'If she told you you're going to have three husbands and ten children,' he told her, 'then watch out, my girl.'

'She said he'd either be dark or fair,' April said quietly, watching his face when she spoke. 'But I never heard which it was to be because you timed it badly and interrupted her.'

Nick grinned. 'Maybe it's as well,' he said.

It gave April an oddly uneasy feeling when she thought about the old gypsy woman's accuracy in forecasting the death of Nick's mother and she wondered just what she would have revealed in store for April herself if Nick had not come along when he did.

She sat for some time over her breakfast that morning, musing about yesterday's not uneventful happenings. She expected Nick had long since been down to look at the new mare they had bought yesterday and he had remarked on her tardiness when she was late down for breakfast. He would by now probably be out somewhere on one of the horses instead of waiting for her as he often did. Nick would never win any prizes for patience.

She looked up, rather startled, when Widgeon appeared in the doorway, looking uneasy in the unaccustomed surroundings as he always did indoors. April frowned curiously. 'Is something wrong, Widgeon?' she asked. 'If you're looking for Mr. Lawton he's been gone some time.'

'I know, miss.' The man shifted his feet uneasily. 'I saw him go out, but somebody'll have to come.'

April put down her coffee cup, a flutter of some unknown dread stirring uneasily in her stomach. 'What's happened?' she asked as she got to her feet.

'It's the colt, miss.' Her head came up sharply and she came across to where he stood just inside the door.

'Starlight?' She knew it was even before he nodded his head, and she swallowed hard on the fear that now sat like a solid lump in her throat. 'Where is he?'

'He's in the drive, miss.'

'You mean he's got out of the paddock and you can't get him back?' Relief sounded in her voice.

'No, miss, he's hurt.'

April was out of the room and the house almost too fast for the man to keep up with her and she ran the last few yards when she saw the small, still shape of Starlight lying on the grass edge of the drive.

It was so unusual to see him still for very long, and she felt the prickle of tears as she knelt beside him and rubbed a soothing and exploratory hand over the silky coat, 'I should have called the vet,' she said, wise too late. 'Widgeon, run back to the house and ring for Mr. Corvet, tell him it's urgent. How did it happen?' she added, as he turned away, and Widgeon looked even more uneasy.

'It was Miss Graves,' he told her slowly. 'She hit him with her car.'

April dismissed him, her mind stunned for the moment

with the thought of anyone so callous as to knock down a young animal and leave it unattended by the roadside. Anger and pity for the colt fought for precedence and she was unsure which was uppermost when Widgeon returned with the news that Mr. Corvet would be along as soon as he could.

It would not be so bad, April thought, if only she did not feel so helpless. She dared not try to move him in case he was badly hurt, and she could only stay there beside him and offer what comfort she could until help arrived.

Widgeon disappeared, about some business of his own, presumably, but it was only a few minutes afterwards that Nick came along and she welcomed him with a woebegone face and a few uncontrollable tears as he knelt beside her.

His strong, gentle fingers explored the colt's thin legs and body and it was only a few minutes before he smiled reassuringly at April as he straightened up. 'I don't think there's too much wrong with him,' he told her confidently. 'But we may as well see what the vet has to say now that he's on his way.'

'But — he's so still,' April objected. 'He must be hurt.'

'He is hurt,' he agreed, 'but I think he's only bruised and shaken. Widgeon says it was only a glancing blow and not really a collision.'

'It was wicked and — and callous to leave him here in the drive without someone to stay with him,' April declared angrily, her eyes bright blue and sparkling anger. She did not care if Fenella Graves was his friend, she was going to say exactly what she thought of her, however much it offended him.

'O.K., it was hard-hearted,' he allowed patiently. 'But Fen would know he wasn't badly hurt.'

'She didn't care if he was or not,' April told him. 'She just drove off and left him.'

'She'd have made sure first that he wasn't badly hurt,' he insisted. 'Fen knows horses and she'd be able to tell as I can.'

'Oh, I knew you'd find excuses for her,' April said crossly. 'I *knew* you would.'

'I'm only being reasonable,' he pointed out quietly.

'Well, I'm not,' she retorted. 'Why didn't she stop? Why did she just drive off and leave the poor little thing there?'

'Now, April—'

'I'll tell you why,' April went on, unheeding anything except her own conviction. 'She wanted Starlight. She wanted you to give him to her for her birthday.'

'Now you're being silly!'

'I'm not being silly, Nick, and you know I'm not.'

'I know you're talking through the back of your head, my girl!' He sounded stern and almost angry, and she told herself that there was no use in expecting him to believe any wrong of Fenella, even if he had refused to let her have Starlight.

'I'm *not*,' she argued, adamant in her conviction. 'She'd made up her mind to have him and when she couldn't she was making sure I didn't have him either.'

'April, stop it!'

She looked at him with wide, reproachful eyes. 'I know you don't want to believe it,' she told him more quietly, 'but she *did* drive off and leave him there without knowing how badly hurt he was.'

'I know it looks bad,' he conceded quietly, 'but it's because you're upset and you're not thinking straight or you'd realize that there was nothing she could have done except get the vet, and she probably sent Widgeon to do just that, only he came for you instead.'

'I – I've been worried sick about him being badly hurt,' April said, and was horrified when two large tears rolled down her dusty cheeks.

Nick pulled her close in a consoling hug, one hand soothing her as he might have done the colt, his voice muffled against her hair. 'Now don't cry about it,' he told her softly. 'You are a girl for making mountains out of molehills, aren't you? Starlight's going to be O.K. and there's no need for anybody to cry, so shush before you frighten poor Starlight even worse.'

She swallowed hastily and raised her head, meeting the gentle laughter in his eyes. 'No matter how I try,' she told him huskily, 'I always seem to end up crying on your shoulder.'

Nick laughed softly, his fingers running through her dark, dishevelled hair. 'What better place to cry?' he asked.

Starlight's recovery was, it seemed to April, almost miraculous and in no time at all she was watching the colt skittering round the paddock with his mother. The fence had been repaired, the hole he had escaped through having been found, and she was even having second thoughts about Fenella's part in the accident.

Nick had spoken to her about it and Fenella had told him that she had, as he guessed, told Widgeon to go and call the vet, but instead he had gone for April. Just the same, April could not imagine herself leaving an injured animal and just driving off.

It was so seldom that Fenella came to Kinley that April had puzzled over it more than once, but when she said as much to her great-uncle he immediately gave her the answer. He did not like the blonde girl and made no secret of it, nor did he like Nick consorting with her and he made no secret of that either, but Nick, as always, went his own way and brooked no interference.

'Do you think you could bear to be parted from your baby for a whole day?' Nick asked her at dinner one Saturday evening, and she looked up curiously.

'I expect I could manage it. Why?'

He grinned. 'I feel like a trip to the coast tomorrow,' he said. 'I thought you might like to come too.'

'I'd love to, but—' She hastily lowered her eyes, and heard Nick laugh as she resumed her meal.

'*But* – you're wondering if Don Jordan will be coming to take you speeding in one of his monsters,' he guessed, and April flushed.

'Or more likely why you aren't taking Fenella Graves to the coast,' she countered.

'Or why you two can't carry on a conversation without arguing,' Simon Carver told them shortly, and frowned when they burst into laughter.

'I'm sorry, Uncle Simon,' April said, 'but it's practically impossible.'

'So I've discovered,' the old man retorted. 'And Nick at least is old enough to know better.'

Nick made a face at April. 'I can't help it, Pop,' he informed the old man gravely. 'She brings out the worst in me.' The face he made at her was so ferocious that she giggled. 'Will you come tomorrow?' he asked. 'Or are you too scared?'

She shook her head. 'I told you – I'd love to come,' she said. 'Just where are we thinking of going?'

'Mayfleet,' he answered promptly. 'I haven't been there since I was a very small boy and I fancy revisiting my boyhood haunts. I'm not even sure how to get there, but I presume you're capable of reading a map?'

'I've never tried,' April informed him airily, 'but I'll try anything once.'

'And that,' Nick said for her ears alone, 'is a challenge if ever I heard one.'

CHAPTER EIGHT

APRIL felt fairly confident that she could cope with the job of navigator even though Nick expressed doubts about her ability. 'I wish you'd stop treating me like a not very bright moron,' she told him as they prepared to leave.

'I don't want you to take on more than you can cope with,' Nick informed her with a grin. 'One hears some hair-raising tales of lady map-readers on rallies and such like, but if you think you can cope, fair enough.'

They took a picnic lunch with them and hoped to be able to pick up some liquid refreshment en route. It was a warm, summery day and April felt undeniably light-hearted as she waved good-bye to her great-uncle, then settled down to enjoy the first part of the trip when her navigation would not be required.

Nick, so he informed her, knew the way as far as Little Merrydown, but after that he would need guidance from the map. 'I suspect that's the only reason you've brought me,' she told him, leaning back in her seat with her eyes closed, feeling unutterably lazy and sleepy. 'Because you needed a navigator.'

'I was rather hoping you wouldn't guess,' Nick said solemnly. 'Knowing how touchy you are.'

'I am *not* touchy,' she denied, without even bothering to open her eyes. 'I've long resigned myself to the fact that you regard me as nothing but a general dogsbody.'

'Oh no,' he denied. 'Not a dogsbody, definitely not.'

April opened her eyes and looked at him suspiciously when she heard him chuckle. 'No?'

He glanced at her from the corners of his eyes and

lowered one lid briefly. 'Oh no. A body, yes, and a very delightful one, but not a dogsbody.'

'You,' April declared firmly, 'have a one-track mind, Nick Lawton.'

'Very likely,' he agreed blandly. 'But look what a lot of fun I have.'

'Do you?' April closed her eyes again. 'I wouldn't know. You professed yourself a virtual saint when I suggested something of the sort.'

'I have never in my life,' Nick declared indignantly, 'professed to be a saint – heaven forbid!'

'You were highly indignant when I told you – suggested to you that your success with women was public knowledge.' She chose her words carefully, but even so they sounded stilted and rather prissy.

'I told you I objected to Don Jordan gossiping about my private business,' he argued. 'That's quite a different matter from claiming to be a saint.'

'Well, whatever it was you meant to sound like, it sounded as if you were denying—'

'I told you I didn't have to deny anything,' he told her quietly. 'I told you it didn't concern anyone but me what I do with my life, and it doesn't, unless—' He cocked a brow at her.

'I'm not interested,' April said hastily, and fell silent.

Little Merrydown proved to be as delightful as its name and so tempting a spot to explore that April insisted they stop and look around it before going on. Much to her surprise, he complied without fuss and they walked around the tiny village hand in hand like a couple of youngsters.

'I can't imagine you in the big city,' he told her as they leaned against a willow tree that swept into the river and lent a welcome shade after the hot sun. 'You look so much at home in the truly rural type of setting.'

April smiled, feeling indeed, as if she belonged to this sort of life. 'I prefer the country,' she admitted. 'But needs must when the devil drives.'

'The devil being Aunt Betty?' he guessed, and she shook her head hastily.

'Oh dear, no! Aunt Betty is a darling, but I have to eat and, unfortunately, I like jam on my bread. There are more jobs that provide jam in London than there are in most small places, so that's where I go.'

'A right little mercenary, in other words,' Nick taunted, and laughed when she looked indignant.

'Not mercenary,' she denied. 'You don't have to think of the pennies, Nick, I do.'

'Don't sound so much like a poor relation, my sweet,' he drawled. 'You know you'll be a rich woman one day and I'm quite sure you'll know how to spend it as well as the next woman.'

'I expect I shall,' April agreed, feeling some of the pleasure going out of the moment when she was reminded of what must happen before she *was* a rich woman. 'I – I don't want to think about being rich,' she told him, leaving the shelter of the tree and walking off alone. 'I don't like what has to happen first.'

Nick caught her up and bent his head to kiss her forehead lightly, holding her hand tightly again. 'Then don't think about it,' he said softly. 'Let's just forget everything and everybody for today and have fun.'

He made it sound so easy, she thought, but it was just beginning to dawn on her that each day brought nearer the time when she must leave Kinley and go back to town. There were so many reasons why she did not want to think about that.

'Now,' he told her a few minutes later as they got back into the car, 'I indulged you in your appetite for rural tranquillity, it's time you earned your keep. Here's the map, that's the road we're on, and all you have to do is watch for the turning, which I've marked with a pencil cross and we should be in Mayfleet in plenty of time for lunch.'

'Hmm.' She studied the tracery of blue and brown lines as he started up the car again. 'It doesn't look too difficult.'

'I'm glad you think so,' he told her. 'Just don't get too confident, that's all.'

They joined a bigger, more busy road and April eyed the constant stream of speeding traffic with disfavour. 'I'll be glad when we leave the main road,' she remarked, and Nick laughed.

'The trouble with you is that you want jam on it all the time,' he told her. 'You go careering about all over the place in those juggernauts of Don's, but you glare at other people who do the same.'

'I'm not glaring at them,' she objected. 'I just don't like busy roads, that's all.'

'Well, keep your eyes peeled,' he warned. 'We should be turning off soon, I think.'

April frowned for a second or two over her map. 'Second turning on the right after the cross-roads,' she said.

The cross-roads safely negotiated, she kept a sharp look out for their turning, and jabbed a finger at the windscreen when she spotted a narrow lane, little more than a cart track, off to the right.

'This one?' Nick sounded doubtful, but she nodded vigorously.

'That's the second turning right,' she insisted. 'The one you've marked with a pencil cross.'

'O.K., you're the navigator.' He turned the car off the main road and drove along the narrow lane, gritty surfaced and hedged on both sides with a thick growth of what she, as a child, had termed 'bread and cheese'. There was also a deep ditch one side and what looked like endless stretches of nothing but corn on both sides. There had been some rain lately and the grass edges beside the lane looked muddy and slippery, while the ripe corn waved, heavy-headed, in the hot sun.

'It's a gorgeous day,' April said. 'Just right for a day by the sea.'

'Hmm.' He gave his attention to the road in front of them, a faint frown pulling at his brows. 'If we ever get there.'

'What do you mean?' She glanced at his face, a faint niggle of doubt gnawing uneasily at the back of her mind.

'I mean, my pretty addle-pate,' Nick said slowly, 'that I don't think this road is likely to get us to Mayfleet. In fact I'm damned sure it won't.'

'But it must do,' April insisted. 'It was the second turning on the right past the cross-roads, the one you'd marked. It must get there eventually.'

He carefully turned another corner and slowed the car to a halt just short of a disused barn that straddled the way ahead, while April stared at it unbelievingly. Nick cut the engine and, in the ensuing silence, she heard him sigh deeply, resting his chin on a hand, the elbow propped on the steering wheel.

'I hate to say I told you so,' he remarked. 'But I did, didn't I?'

'But I don't understand it,' April protested, looking at the derelict barn as if it had suddenly materialized out of thin air. 'The road *must* go somewhere, it can't just go nowhere.'

'In the English countryside it can,' Nick assured her. 'The eccentricities of English road-builders are world-famous, not to mention those of girl map-readers.'

'But it's – it's idiotic,' she insisted.

'I agree.' He leaned across and took the map from her, studied it for a moment, then looked at her with an expression she could not interpret but which looked as if it boded ill for somebody.

'Nick?'

'As you're a rank amateur,' he said slowly, 'I have made allowances, but even you've excelled yourself this time.'

He held out the map for her to look at and she studied it for a second before shaking her head. 'I don't—' she began.

'It's always more accurate if you read it the right way up,' he told her. April stared at it wide-eyed, her hands to her mouth. 'You pudden-headed, screwy little—' He sighed deeply. 'You've had the blessed thing upside down. We should have turned left two turnings back before the crossroads, not second right after them.'

'I'm — I'm sorry, Nick.' She felt small and guilty and she would not really have blamed him if he had been more angry about it.

'I'm undecided,' he said, ignoring the apology, 'whether to strangle you and dump you here in that nice deep, muddy pitch, or whether to simply abandon you here in the middle of nowhere and let you find your own way home.'

'Oh, Nick, I really *am* sorry.' She had no qualms at all about using her eyes to look as appealing as possible. 'I'd never make it on my own,' she said woefully, 'not with my sense of direction.'

He studied her for a moment with his tip-tilted, unfathomable eyes, then he smiled at last and shook his head slowly. 'You look as soulful as a kitten on a calendar,' he told her, 'so I suppose I'd better let you get away with it this time.'

'We — we could turn round and go back,' she suggested meekly.

'We could,' he agreed, 'if we have room to manoeuvre the car in this narrow lane. We have a choice of three exits. We can drive straight at the barn and finish off the demolition job, mow down a couple of yards of the farmer's crop or take our chance on that ditch, and I think it had better be the latter. I might just make it.'

He restarted the engine, while April sat small and silent beside him. There was very little room to turn and she held her breath as they got nearer and nearer the edge of the ditch. Three times Nick reversed and then drove forward again and it began to look as if they would manage it without incident, when a very slight miscalculation sent them slithering down into the muddy ditch, the rear wheels spinning hopelessly in the thick water while the front tipped slowly upwards.

'Well,' Nick cut the engine, 'that's it.'

'We're stuck?'

'We're stuck,' he echoed, sitting back and apparently resigned. 'We are well and truly stuck, my little genius.'

'I knew you'd say it was my fault,' she said dolefully. 'What can we do, Nick?'

He looked at her for a second with a wicked gleam in his eyes, then scanned the surrounding acres of corn. 'Well now, let's see. I can see some chimneys just across there, and that no doubt means a farmhouse, so one of us can trek across there and ask, very nicely, if we can use the telephone. O.K.?'

April nodded uneasily. 'You – you want me to go?' she ventured.

'Oh, I think you ought to, don't you?' He sounded quite serious and she did not meet his eyes, so she did not see the glint of amusement that met her suggestion.

Without a word she opened the car door, but before she could even swing her feet out over the muddy ground, he leaned across and closed it again, his laugh warm and reassuring close to her ear. 'You little crackpot, you really are in a masochistic mood, aren't you?' he teased. 'Of course you won't go, I will. You stay here while I plough my way through the corn – and don't let anybody steal you while I'm gone.'

April looked around the seemingly endless acres of corn, the ramshackle barn and the sheer loneliness of the place. 'Please, Nick – can't I come with you?' she begged.

'Scared?' An arched brow recognized her weakness. 'O.K., come on, then.'

It was a little damp underfoot, but the sun was warm and a lark somewhere serenaded them as they followed a narrow path through the corn. She followed Nick, his hand holding hers, and only realized how far they had come when they reached a stile into a meadow and she looked back.

'Nearly there,' Nick encouraged as he lifted her down from the stile. 'Enjoying your walk?'

She nodded. 'As a matter of fact I am,' she said. 'It's rather lovely walking through a cornfield. Quite—'

'Romantic?' he suggested softly, and laughed when she shook her head.

'Nick, will we still have time to go to the coast?'

'It depends,' he demurred. 'If the car's O.K. and we can find some co-operative garage man to rescue it for us, then we can. If not—' He shrugged, and April looked at him anxiously.

'If not?' she prompted, and he looked down at her steadily, smiling.

'Then there's always another time,' he said.

'I wouldn't blame you if you wouldn't bring me again,' she told him, determined to be the villain of the piece.

'Neither would I,' he declared frankly, and laughed when she pouted reproachfully, hugging her against him and shaking his head. 'Poor April,' he teased, 'you *are* feeling sorry for yourself, aren't you?'

'I'm wondering how we'll get back if the car can't be recovered today,' she ventured.

He shrugged. 'I don't know. Maybe we'll have to wait until morning.'

'Oh no, Nick!' Too late she realized he was not serious and her heart was already hammering distressingly hard against her ribs. 'There must be buses,' she said, the colour high in her cheeks. 'There's bound to be one going somewhere.'

Nick raised a doubting brow. 'On a Sunday?' he asked. 'In the country? I should think it's very unlikely.'

'Well – well a taxi, then. There must be some way of getting out of this place, even on a Sunday.'

He responded by humming a chorus of 'Never on Sunday', which did nothing to help at all, and April felt very much like giving up in despair.

The farmhouse at first looked deserted, but then, as Nick raised a hand to knock on the door, a man appeared from the back of the house, eyeing them curiously, and Nick smiled hopefully at him.

'I'm sorry to trouble you,' he told him, 'but our car's in a ditch the other side of that cornfield, and I wondered if we could use your phone to call a garage.'

The man nodded his head, apparently in sympathy, his narrow, weather-paled eyes missing nothing of April's short, sleeveless dress and her long slim legs. 'Took the wrong turning, did you?' he asked, and half-smiled when Nick nodded agreement. 'Well, tain't first time it's bin done and 'twon't be the last, I expect. Never 'ad nobody go in the ditch before, though,' he mused. 'It'll be muddy, I expect.'

'Very,' Nick agreed dryly. 'If we *could* use your phone, Mr. —'

'Brown,' the man supplied promptly. 'You could use the phone an' welcome,' he added, ''cept I ain't got one.'

'Ah well,' Nick sighed resignedly, 'that's that.'

April's mind was already racing ahead to other possible means of escape from the place. It was inconceivable that they should be stranded there as Nick had suggested, but she looked up briefly and caught him watching her with that bright, speculative gleam in his eyes again and hastily looked away.

'Are there buses?' he asked, and the farmer shook his head.

'Not on Sundays, mister, never.'

'And no way of summoning a taxi,' Nick said. 'Even supposing there was one within a radius of ten miles, so it looks as if we're well and truly stuck, my love.'

The endearment brought the man's sharp eyes in her direction again. 'I 'spect the young lady could do with a nice cuppa tea, eh, my dear?'

'That's a good idea,' Nick told him, before April could answer for herself. 'You go and have a cup of tea while I hike down to the nearest garage and try and rout somebody out to help us.'

April looked doubtful, and her doubt showed quite plainly on her face, although she did not at first realize it. The farmer's eyes went from one to the other and he smiled knowingly. 'I don't reckon that'll be necessary,' he said. 'For one thing your young lady don't fancy bein' left 'ere on her own, do you, my dear?'

'Oh no, please don't misunderstand—' April began, but the man chuckled knowingly and shook his head.

'I don't mind, my dear. 'Tis somethin' of a compliment to an old duffer like me, I reckon, when a lovely young lady don't like to be left alone wi' me, but there's no need for anybody to go down the village for the breakdown

126

less'n you'd rather. I got a tractor I can haul you out with easy enough, I reckon.'

Nick grinned. 'Thanks,' he said. 'I'm sure there's no damage, if we could just get it free we can go on our way.'

The man nodded. 'But first we'll all 'ave that sup of tea,' he told him. 'Come on in.'

The farmer, it transpired, lived alone and he was reluctant to part with his unexpected guests, so that it was some time before he could be persuaded to leave their friendly tea and get out the tractor. Nick and April agreed to walk back the way they had come, while the tractor was driven round by the road, and their host grinned at them as they prepared to start out.

'If'n we can't shift the old car after I've hauled it out of the ditch,' he said, 'I got room to put folk up, if you've a mind to.'

'Have you?' Nick looked interested, and April stared at him in disbelief. 'Well, if we can't get going, Mr. Brown, maybe we'll take you up on that.'

The man's eyes gleamed with such salacious glee that April could feel the colour in her cheeks. 'There's a nice big room could soon be made ready,' he said, and winked at Nick broadly.

'Thanks – I'll remember that.'

'That *won't* be necessary, thank you,' April told him firmly, giving Nick the most withering look she could summon. 'We'll get back somehow, even if I have to walk all the way back.'

The man chuckled as he went off to fetch the tractor and April refused to take Nick's hand as they started across the meadow to the cornfield, her colour and her chin high. They walked in silence for some time, and the lark sounded somehow less tuneful than shrill to April this time.

'Now what have I done?' Nick asked after a while, and sought and found her hand, holding too tightly for her to free it as she tried to.

'You know quite well, Nick.'

He laughed softly, and squeezed the hand he held. 'Oh, I see, because I told the old feller we might take advantage of his generous offer of bed and board for the night.'

'You needn't have—'

'You think I meant it, don't you?'

She did not look at him for a moment, but down at the narrow path they trod, her heart skipping wildly as she considered the possibility of him being serious. 'You sounded serious,' she told him.

'What would you have done if it had come to the point?' he asked quietly, and she looked up then.

There was something infinitely puzzling about Nick and she could not, at this moment, determine whether he was just teasing her as he so often did or if he was genuinely serious. 'You – you know quite well what I'd do, Nick.'

He smiled slowly, his unfathomable eyes travelling over her face in a way that set her pulses racing faster than ever. 'I know,' he said quietly. 'But I had to try my notorious woman-killing powers, didn't I?'

So that was it, she thought; he had in his own way been paying her back for believing the reputation Donald had credited him with. But she was still horribly uncertain whether or not he had meant it, and whether or not Donald was right about him. It was a mystery that sat uneasily in her mind all the way back to the car and long afterwards.

It took little effort on the part of the tractor to free the car from the muddy ditch and April watched as the two men examined it for damage. Apparently satisfied that nothing was wrong except a coating of mud, Nick thanked the helpful farmer and they made their way back along the narrow lane to the main road.

April was so very quiet that Nick glanced at her curiously once or twice before remarking on it. 'Do I read disapproval in your stony silence?' he asked at last.

'If you like.'

He raised a brow. 'Why, for heaven's sake? You can't still be brooding over that bit of nonsense with our farmer friend – or are you?'

April flushed, recalling the man's sharp, speculative eyes when he had made the suggestion to Nick and her own unconcealable embarrassment. 'You may have thought it was amusing,' she told him, 'but it made me look a – a fool. A naïve fool at that.'

He laughed the idea to scorn. 'Nothing of the sort,' he denied. 'If you'd played up, as I did, no one would have taken any notice.'

She glared at him indignantly. 'Forgive me if I don't fall into the role of experienced *femme fatale* with as much ease as some of your – your friends do,' she said. 'You should have known I'd—'

'Blow your top?' he suggested inelegantly and a little impatiently, she thought. 'Yes, I should have guessed you would, my sweet. You're a great gal for letting off the fireworks whenever your dignity's threatened.'

'Well, can you blame me?' she demanded, reasonably, she thought. 'Heaven knows what that farmer thought.'

'Oh, don't worry about Farmer Brown,' he told her. 'He could read between the lines.'

'No doubt,' April retorted rashly. 'I'm sure he read *you* correctly.'

She saw the small, almost imperceptible tightening of

his mouth and the slight frown that drew his dark brows together. 'I ought to do something horrible to you for that,' he told her quietly, 'and I probably will.' He laughed then and turned a swift, speculative glance on her. 'Or maybe I should do something to Don Jordan instead,' he added. 'After all, he put those nasty ideas into your head in the first place.'

He sounded cross, she thought, and she regretted it more than she was prepared to admit. It had promised to be such a wonderful day, and now she was quarrelling with Nick and it could so easily be disastrous. Perhaps it had been only a rather ribald joke and she had been a mite more touchy than she need have been about it.

'Nick.' It was not easy to eat humble pie, but she hated to see their whole day spoiled by one small incident. 'I'm – I'm sorry.'

He said nothing for a moment, then he took one hand off the steering wheel and laid it briefly over hers, his smile rueful but still teasing. 'Never mind,' he said. 'Let's forget it and just enjoy ourselves, shall we?'

April nodded, but somewhere at the back of her mind, the intriguing thought persisted – whether or not he had been as serious about the suggestion as he had appeared to be. Hastily she decided it was not the sort of thing she should think about too much.

CHAPTER NINE

APRIL was just a little uncertain of her new mount and rode only very slowly across the meadow. April Girl, the mare Nick had bought at Pickett Fair, was more frisky than either of the other two horses she was used to and she had never been allowed to take her out before. This morning, however, she had persuaded Nick to let her try the mare and he had, rather unwilling, agreed. Now she wondered if she had been too rash, especially as Nick was not along to keep an eye on her.

The mare gave the impression that she would like nothing better than to kick up her heels and expend some of her surplus energy; instead she was obliged to walk sedately and her small head tossed disapprovingly at the tedium of it.

They went across the meadow, as usual, and took the path that curved round behind a small wood and hid Kinley from view for some fifty yards. It always gave April a sense of isolation when she rode round behind the wood, a sensation she quite enjoyed sometimes, with no sign of human habitation until Jordan's came into sight on the other side of the stream and half hidden by a rise in the ground.

She rode alone this morning because Nick had business with a neighbouring farmer, so he said, about the non-delivery of some hay. Whether he also hoped to see Fenella Graves while he was out was a question that April considered musingly. Not, she told herself, that she cared about it either way.

There was a brisk breeze that tossed her hair about her face and whipped bright colour into her cheeks, and she was managing the mare far better than she had hoped, although she was undoubtedly strong and wilful. The trees thinned after a while and the ground sloped down towards the stream, then opened out on the other side of the wood to a steep, lush meadow.

Leaving the trees and emerging again into the open, April caught sight of another rider coming towards her. It was not Nick, as she had half expected, but Fenella Graves. There was no mistaking the pale blonde hair, so smoothly dressed, even in the brisk wind that blew in across the open ground. The tall almost masculine figure, in breeches and shirt, sat straight and confident in the saddle and she must have seen April, although she gave no sign that she had.

Some eighty or ninety yards separated them and Fenella rode straight towards her, giving no sign of greeting until she was close enough for April to see the sharp, speculative look in the hazel eyes. Then April remembered that Fenella too had bid for the mare that she was riding, and lost to Nick. Fenella was not a woman who willingly lost to anyone and the mare was the second disappointment she had suffered where April was concerned.

'Good morning, Fenella.' They were close enough now to make it impossible for April to ignore her, much as she was tempted.

Fenella, however, had no such social obligations to politeness and she did not even bother with the usual brief nod which was her normal form of greeting whenever they met. Her attention was centred entirely on the animal she coveted, and she had no interest at all in the rider.

'Does Nick know you're riding that mare?' she asked abruptly and without preamble, and April instinctively raised her chin defiantly.

'Of course he knows,' she said.

Fenella's lip curled as she recognized her difficulty in holding the restless mare. 'I'm surprised he hadn't more sense,' she told her. 'Are you capable of handling it?'

April flushed. 'Quite capable, thank you. I should hardly have taken her if I wasn't.'

A short humourless laugh greeted that reply and April bit her lip angrily. 'I'm not so sure,' Fenella jeered. 'You have a habit of biting off a bit more than you can chew, haven't you?'

As if to prove her right, the mare decided to take things into her own hands for a minute or two and April fought to control her as she went round and round, trying to free her mouth of the bit.

'As you can see,' April said at last, a little breathlessly, 'I can manage her, and I haven't bitten off more than I can chew.'

'You've coped so far,' Fenella told her shortly, possibly disappointed she had not been thrown, 'but I wouldn't guarantee you getting back.' A small, sly smile goaded April's anger. 'It seems to me that you're no more successful with a spirited horse than you are with a man.'

'I—' April began, but was cut short by that harsh, confident voice again.

'Don't deny it,' Fenella told her. 'You've tried hard enough to make Nick notice you, with your stupid clumsiness and childishness, but it won't work, you know. Nick sees through your pathetic tricks easily. You may have got away with it seven years ago, but not now.'

Fingers white-knuckled, April clung to the rein, her blue eyes blazing furiously at this woman who seemed so determined to make her lose her temper. 'You seem to know a lot more of my intentions than I do myself, Miss Graves,' she said. 'And I really have no desire to stand here and indulge in a slanging exchange with you.'

She would have ridden off then, but Fenella had other ideas, apparently, for she put out a hand and gripped the rein, making it impossible for her to go, while the mare shook her head at this new sign of authority.

'Not so fast,' Fenella told her. 'I haven't finished with you yet, *Miss* Summers.'

'I've nothing to say to you,' April told her, still clinging to her self-control, though only with difficulty.

'Well, I have something to say to you,' Fenella informed her. 'I know you imagine you have some sort of relationship with Nick, but I know differently.'

'I don't claim any sort of relationship, as you call it,' April denied. 'Except the legal one which makes us some sort of distant cousins, I suppose. I've known Nick a long time, that's all.'

Fenella's sharp eyes swept over her scornfully. 'And you had a schoolgirl crush on him,' she jeered. 'Everyone knows about *that* little episode.'

It was more and more difficult to remain rational but, April told herself, if anyone was going to lose her temper and make a fool of herself it was going to be Fenella Graves. *She* intended maintaining her dignity at all costs. She tipped back her head and looked down her small nose at her tormentor.

'I outgrew that years ago,' she said, with what she considered was admirable restraint. 'Everyone knows *that* too.'

'Do they?' The hazel eyes gleamed like polished amber. 'I've watched you with Nick, and I'm not fooled, nor is Nick.' April looked at her warily, suddenly uneasy, and Fenella pressed home her advantage. 'He laughs at you, didn't you realize that? He finds you a constant source of amusement, and pathetically schoolgirlish. You don't stand a chance with a man like Nick, and it's time you realized it. Stick to Donald Jordan, he's more your style.'

April's head swam with a thousand angry retorts, but she could think of nothing sufficiently crushing until she remembered her quite eventful trip to Mayfleet with Nick, the previous Sunday. That had been none of her doing, in fact it could be quite fairly said that he had talked her into it. He had stopped in the tiny village of Little Merrydown simply because she had wanted to see it, and as for his behaviour at the farm – well, that would surely open Fenella Graves' eyes if she knew of it.

She half-smiled as she looked at Fenella. 'If Nick has such a low opinion of me, Miss Graves,' she said with deceptive mildness, 'why do you suppose it was me he persuaded to go to Mayfleet with him on Sunday?' She noted, with satisfaction, the brief flick of surprise in the hazel eyes. 'Or didn't you know about that?' she added softly.

The ensuing silence was answer enough. Obviously Fenella had known nothing about Nick's outing with her and the news not only surprised but angered her. The sharp hazel eyes studied her narrowly and the knuckles of the hand holding the rein were white.

'You're lying,' Fenella said tightly, and April shook her head.

'I'm not lying,' she denied. 'But if you don't believe *me*, why not ask Nick yourself?'

'You—' The set features contorted in a brief second's loss of control and her eyes blazed furiously. 'If you know what's good for you,' she said, ominously quiet, 'you'll go back where you belong before you get hurt.'

April was feeling as if she had the upper hand at last and the temptation to rub salt in the wound was too much to resist. 'Why?' she asked.

For a moment the question seemed to puzzle Fenella, then she narrowed her eyes, her mouth tight and thin.

'Because Nick isn't your type,' she said. 'You don't stand a chance of making him fall seriously for that childish manner of yours, and you may as well face the fact.'

The idea of Nick falling seriously for her had, April admitted, not really entered her head until now, but a challenge was a challenge, and she lifted her chin, a small, tight smile just touching her mouth. 'If that's the case, Miss Graves,' she said softly, 'why are you so worried about my staying here?'

She drew an involuntary breath at the viciousness of the look she received, and wondered at her own rashness. 'Damn you!' Fenella said between her teeth, and without warning she released the rein she held and brought her riding crop down sharply across the impatient mare's rump.

April Girl, like her rider, was anxious to be away, but the crop stung sharply and she was already very annoyed at being kept standing so long, so that given the chance, she took off like the wind. Racing back across the open ground towards the trees and into the wood without pause, only a miracle keeping April still in the saddle.

Low branches snatched at her, and whipped back as the mare sped over the loamy ground recklessly, the bit firmly between her teeth at last. Out into the open the other side of the wood and careering across the meadow as if the devil was after her, with April clinging on desperately.

It was worse, much worse, than when Dingo had taken her racing up the slope to escape from Nick, and this time Nick was not close at hand as he had been then. She was uncertain whether or not to be glad of the latter. Certainly if he had been there he would no doubt have thought, yet again, that she was accident-prone, even though this was none of her doing.

Fenella Graves' words came to her again, as she clung

on grimly and hoped for the best, that her stupid clumsiness had been deliberately contrived to make Nick take notice of her. Surely this was proof enough that she had no need to contrive situations; her own natural disposition towards events of this kind were all too frequent. Her only worry was, at the moment, whether Nick shared Fenella's opinion that she got into trouble deliberately.

She half-turned her head, aware of someone else coming up from her right. Another figure on horseback, but unrecognizable in the brief, blurred glimpse she had of it. All her strength and energy was concentrated on trying to regain control of her mount, although she feared she had little chance now that the mare had the bit.

She found herself wishing desperately that it could be Donald coming across the meadow, since he would not be likely to share the view that the fault was hers. Only something she had no control over knew instinctively that it would be Nick, and that he would reach her before the mare managed to unseat her. The same instinct that dragged a faint despairing cry from her that sounded pitifully thin on the wind that was whipped up by their speed.

'Nick!'

She could now just distinguish the reassuring sound of hooves on the ground as she kept her head up and hung on tight to the mare's flying mane, but it seemed like hours before the other animal came near enough and she dared not turn her head to see who it was.

'Let go!' Nick's blessedly familiar voice yelled at her. 'Kick your feet free!'

'I can't, Nick!' The thought of being on that flying fury of muscle without the balance of her feet in stirrups turned her cold.

'Let go!' Nick yelled again. 'Let go, April!'

She felt rather like a car driver who closes his eyes and

137

hopes for the best, as she obeyed, and a fraction of a second later an arm reached out for her and she was lifted from the saddle and deposited, none too gently, in front of him, where she promptly buried her head against his chest – something she had sworn never to do again.

Her heart was beating wildly and she felt as if she would never walk again because her legs were so weak and trembly, but Nick gave all his attention to quieting his mount. 'Easy, boy, easy!' He coaxed the bay to a halt while the mare went thundering on, although with much less enthusiasm now that her rider was gone and she was deprived of the pleasure of showing who was boss.

The comforting arm still encircled April's waist and Nick's face rested against her hair as she kept her face hidden. He said nothing for several minutes, then a hand raised her chin and curious eyes regarded her pale face and huge, scared eyes. 'Better?' he asked, and she nodded.

'Yes. Yes, I think so.'

'I can't trust you alone with anything, can I?' he asked in a voice as much resigned as annoyed. 'How do you always manage to get yourself into difficulties?' The question reminded her again of Fenella Graves' accusation and she stirred uneasily, moving her chin so that she need not look at him.

'I – I couldn't help it,' she said, and he sighed.

'You never can, but somehow or other you go from one thing to another, don't you?'

'I don't—'

'It's a good job I'm usually around to rescue you,' he went on, ignoring her attempt to deny any deliberate action on her part, 'or heaven knows what grief you'd come to.'

It was that jibe of Fenella's of course that made her ultra-sensitive, but she flushed and hastily lowered her eyes. 'You sound as if you think I do it on purpose,' she complained, and he laughed.

'Do you?'

'Oh no, Nick, of course not!' She looked at him appealingly. 'Please don't believe that.'

The encircling arm hugged her briefly, and he laughed again. 'I don't think anyone would willingly take the sort of chances you do,' he told her. 'For any reason that I can think of.' He looked down at her and smiled wryly. 'I suppose I can take part of the blame for it this time,' he said. 'I shouldn't have let you have the mare, she's too fly for you. I knew you'd never be able to handle her.'

'Oh, but I can,' April protested. 'I was managing perfectly well.'

'Huh!' He raised his eyes to heaven in appeal. 'Listen to her. I was managing perfectly well!'

'So I was,' April insisted. 'Until—'

She hesitated to voice the blame, although when she remembered that humiliating exchange with Fenella she wondered why she was being so reticent.

'Until?' Nick prompted, obviously curious, and she lowered her eyes.

'Until Fenella Graves took a hand,' she told him.

'Fen?' He frowned curiously. 'Where does she come into it?'

'She – she panicked April Girl.'

He laughed. 'Which one?' he asked, not taking her seriously obviously.

'I'm serious, Nick. She deliberately panicked the mare.'

He looked down at her, his eyes still as much amused as curious, and she wondered if she was wasting her time trying to explain. 'How and why?' he demanded.

'How is easy,' April said. 'She lost her temper and hit the mare with her crop. She was restless and didn't like standing still for so long and neither of us was expecting it, so—'

'So you both panicked,' he guessed wryly.

'Oh, what's the use?' April said crossly. 'I knew you wouldn't believe it was Fenella's fault. I should have known you'd call me a liar.'

'I did nothing of the sort,' he denied, and his unusual and intriguing eyes looked at her steadily for a moment or two, then he frowned. 'What I don't understand is why she should do such a stupid thing, when she must have known you wouldn't be able to handle the mare if she was frightened.'

April looked down at her hands, feeling the colour in her cheeks and wishing he was not so embarrassingly close and able to watch her expression so easily. If he knew what Fenella had said about her trying to draw his attention to herself, he would probably laugh, but April would find it unbearable.

'I – I don't know,' she said, and his hand lifted her chin again so that she was more or less obliged to look at him, see him frowning.

'When you hang your head and say things like that,' he informed her, 'I get suspicious. I don't believe you – why would Fenella do anything as stupid as trying to break your pretty neck? She doesn't do anything without a reason.'

'Exactly,' April said, moving out of his hold again and studiously looking at her hands.

Nick sighed deeply, and the arm about her waist tightened its hold. 'If you don't explain yourself instead of making oblique implications,' he threatened, 'I'll do you an injury, April, I swear it.'

'Oh, don't pretend you don't know,' April declared. 'I'm not the one who's being obtuse, Nick, it's you!'

'Maybe,' he agreed unrelentingly, 'so you explain.'

'She's – she's—' She swallowed hard. It would be too humiliating, if Fenella was right about his opinion of her, to tell him that the other girl was jealous. 'She doesn't like us – like me being friendly with you,' she managed at last, and bit hard on her lip when his laughter vibrated against her.

'That,' he declared flatly, 'is the most idiotic thing I ever heard.'

'I know it is,' she said, wishing desperately that she could escape and run somewhere and hide her face. Anywhere rather than stay perched in front of him with his arm encircling her waist while he laughed at the idea of Fenella's need to be jealous of her.

'What did you say to her that made her blow her top?' he inquired inelegantly. 'You must have said something,' he added when she looked like arguing.

'I – I only mentioned that we – I'd been to Mayfleet with you last Sunday,' she admitted, and he laughed again, shaking his head slowly.

'You little pussy,' he said, his eyes glinting wickedly as if the whole idea amused him intensely. 'You love putting the cat among the pigeons, don't you?'

'No, I don't,' April denied indignantly. She could see now that Fenella's action could probably be attributed to her rash jibe and she wanted the subject closed once and for all before it became any more embarrassing. 'Let me down,' she told him, her nose in the air. 'I have to catch April Girl.'

He looked up and across to where the mare stood, grazing spasmodically, but keeping a wary eye on them. 'There's no need,' he told her. 'I'll get her.' He swung himself down from the saddle and left her in sole possession. 'You ride this fellow back to Kinley,' he said. 'You shouldn't have any trouble with him, I've run most of the skittishness out of him.'

'But—' She looked down at him, his strong face showing a determination she knew she could not argue with.

'I'll get her,' he insisted. 'You leave her to me, she won't try any nonsense with me, she knows better.'

'Nick—' He looked up at her inquiringly and the question died on her lips. How could she ask him not to be too harsh with her namesake? He would probably laugh at her again and she did not think she could stand the humiliation of that again so soon.

If Donald noticed that she was rather quieter than usual that evening, he made no comment on it and April sat beside him, rather absently thoughtful, as they sped along the quiet roads.

It was a lovely, tranquil sort of evening and gradually she relaxed. In the open car they created a welcome wind and she leaned back her head and watched the hedges skim by and the white-streaked sky drift lazily above them.

'I could go on for ever,' she said, turning her head to look at Donald, and he smiled.

'Shall we?' he asked, without taking his eyes off the road. Since their near collision with Nick, he invariably gave his whole attention to the job in hand when he was driving.

'Why not?' she countered. 'Where would we find ourselves, Donald?'

He shook his head. 'Heaven knows, but I was thinking of taking you to a nice little pub I've discovered. If you'd like to come, of course. Would you?'

April nodded. 'I'd love to.'

'I hoped you would.' He chanced a brief look at her over his shoulder. 'As long as you're happy.'

She smiled, looking at the fair, good-looking face and nice grey eyes. Donald was a man any girl would be pleased to be seen with and she wondered just how fond she had grown of him in the weeks she had been at Kinley.

'I'm usually happy,' she said.

'You should be, always.' He sounded so much more serious than she did and she glanced at him again curiously. 'I love you, April.'

He said it solemnly and with every appearance of meaning it, as she had no doubt he did, although it was surely the most unconventional moment to make such an announcement. 'Do – do you?' She was too uncertain of her own feelings to be quite sure how to respond.

'You know I do.'

'I – I suppose I do,' she admitted. 'Although you've never actually said so.'

'But you knew it,' he insisted, and April nodded, finding it even more disconcerting because of the unusual situation she found herself in. Surely flying along a country road in a fast car was not the usual way a girl heard such a pronouncement.

'Yes, Donald, I knew it,' she said.

He was silent for a moment and his expression did not change, as near as she could judge, when he spoke again. 'But you wish I hadn't said it,' he guessed then, and April shook her head.

'Oh, no, not really.'

He said no more for the moment, but slowed down the car and drove it up on to the grass verge in the shade of the hedge, sitting for a moment in the silence before he spoke. 'I *do* love you,' he said then. 'I think I always have, April.'

He leaned across and took her hands in his, his expression serious as ever, and she looked down at their hands rather than at him, feeling a strange, uneasy flutter in her heart as she spoke. 'You must have had girl-friends in between then and now,' she said. 'After all, it was seven years ago that you knew me before, and you were only seventeen then.'

He shook his head. 'I never did have a serious girl-friend,' he confessed. 'I was always so crazy about cars and that took all my time and money when I was younger, then my father died and I had the farm to run singlehanded. Besides,' he added, 'I never *really* got over you the first time, April.'

'It's – it's very touching, and I'm flattered you've been so faithful to my girlish image,' she told him, not meaning to sound facetious, but he frowned.

His fair brows were drawn together above the grey eyes. 'Please, April, don't use Nick's way of speaking. It never sounds sincere.'

'Nick's—' She looked at him uncomprehendingly for a moment, then she shook her head. 'I didn't know it was Nick's way of speaking,' she told him. 'I didn't mean it insincerely, Donald.'

'I know.' His fingers held hers tightly and he leaned forward in his seat, anxious that she should not mis-understand him. 'It's just that being with him so much you do it without thinking, I suppose.'

'I didn't know I sounded like Nick,' she said. 'Do I?'

He seemed not to have heard her, but leaned across and kissed her lightly on her cheek. 'Thank heaven he'll soon be out of circulation for good,' he said. 'Then perhaps I can have you to myself.'

The wish went unnoticed, for April was staring at him with wide, incredulous eyes, her heart thudding hard at her ribs. 'Out of circulation?' she echoed. 'What – what do you mean, Donald?'

He looked at her for a moment in such a way that she could believe he had said more than he had intended, but she could not let it rest now. 'I shouldn't have said any-

thing,' he told her. 'But I – well, I didn't exactly promise
Fenella I wouldn't, so it's O.K., I suppose.' His eyes narrowed for a moment and he looked uncertain. 'I wonder
Nick hasn't told you himelf,' he said. 'He's not usually
reticent about *any*thing much, is he?'

'Donald—'

'They're getting married soon,' Donald said. 'Nick and
Fenella. Didn't you know?'

CHAPTER TEN

DIFFICULT as it was to believe, April knew that Donald was the last person to joke about something like a marriage between Nick and Fenella, so she must believe that there were wedding plans in hand. It was just as hard for her to visualize Nick as the conventional idea of a husband, but no doubt Fenella was quite prepared to accept him as he was.

April remembered how he had laughed at the idea of Fenella being jealous of her, and she could have curled up in shame when she thought of what a fool he must have thought her. As if Fenella had need to be jealous of anyone, least of all April. The thing that hurt most, however, was that Nick had not told her that he was marrying Fenella but had simply laughed at her and told her the idea of jealousy was idiotic.

She hoped Donald would not realize how the news had affected her, and she had been only too eager to accept his renewed invitation to visit some little country inn he knew of. She was not even prepared to face the fact that the news affected her at all, except as a surprise, but somewhere at the back of her mind she knew it had.

She sat now with her second Bloody Mary in her hand, smiling at Donald across the small table in one corner of the lounge bar. There were quite a few customers, but it was possible to create an atmosphere of isolation merely by turning one's back to the rest of the room, and making the quiet hum of voices a mere background to more personal conversation.

Donald looked rather more cheerful than she ever remembered seeing him, and he raised his glass to her with a smile that was unmistakably a compliment. 'To you,' he said quietly. 'The loveliest girl in the world.'

She bowed in mock humility and looked at him from under her lashes. 'I feel like making an evening of it,' she told him rashly, raising her own glass. 'Here's to romance, Donald. Long may it flourish.'

'Amen,' he added piously, and looked at her for a second as if trying to come to a decision. 'I know a club,' he said at last, 'where we could dance and eat if you feel like making an evening of it.'

April laughed. 'Why not?' she said, and looked at him curiously. '*Do* you dance?'

'Don't you remember?' he asked, looking reproachful. 'The first time I ever saw you I asked you to dance with me, and I dreamed about it for months afterwards because you did.'

'Did you?' She put her head on one side, trying hard to remember the old Donald. The seventeen-year-old who had followed her around so adoringly all those years ago. 'I should remember,' she said, 'but I'm ashamed to say I don't. I was only fifteen then, of course,' she added, and he made a rueful face.

'And you had a thing about Nick,' he said.

April nodded, not looking at him. 'And I had a thing about Nick,' she agreed quietly.

'But you haven't any more?' he asked, and sounded anxious to have it confirmed.

She shook her head firmly. 'No, of course not.'

'Then shall we go?'

She blinked at him for a moment, then nodded her head and finished her drink. 'Let's go,' she said.

The club Donald took her to was not the kind of place she had imagined him frequenting, especially in view of his earlier talk of spending all his time and money on cars, but she supposed everyone was allowed a certain amount of licence in such a situation. He seemed, in fact, to be quite well known to a number of people there.

It was a typical country club atmosphere and almost everyone knew everyone else. The bar was crowded, so they took their drinks to a table and as they sat down April realized that she had never visualized Donald as a drinking man either, yet this must be his third whisky since they started out.

There was quite a different atmosphere in the club from that of the little inn they had visited earlier and they were soon involved with a group of people that Donald apparently knew quite well. Another drink was put in front of April and she began to realize that she had had more than enough already, and far more than she normally drank. The room was taking on a slightly unreal look and her head felt alarmingly as if it was floating several feet above her body.

It must be the drink too, she decided a moment later, that made her imagine she saw Nick and Fenella Graves come into the bar, but surely an hallucination would not have frowned so blackly when it saw her, nor would it have changed course and come determinedly across the room towards them with Fenella in reluctant attendance.

The party greeted him with welcoming cries, with the exception of Donald who glared at him balefully as if he suspected him of heaven knows what. Nick acknowledged the greetings, but only half-heartedly, it seemed, for his attention was centred on April and she had the feeling that she was smiling rather vaguely at him.

'Hello, April.' He stood across the other side of the table from her, but she could feel the effect of those strange, tip-tilted eyes even so, and she blinked at him.

'Hello, Nick, join the party.'

'No, thanks, we're not staying long.' He spared Donald a glance and she had to notice the tightness at the corners of his wide mouth. 'It looks like quite a party.'

'We think so,' Donald told him, with far more bravado than he usually displayed, and Nick nodded.

He looked, April thought, as if he was somewhat at a loss, and that too was unusual. He hesitated a moment longer, his gaze on April's flushed cheeks and brilliant blue eyes, then he turned abruptly and walked off, again accompanied by Fenella, who had remained ominously silent. For some reason she could not explain April felt suddenly and dismayingly guilty, and had the most ridiculous urge to get up and follow him, but instead she stayed where she was looking at her drink as if she had quite lost her taste for it.

It was late when they left the club and April was not at all sure that she wanted to drive home with Donald in the state he was. He had had at least two more whiskies and he had an air of swaggering bravado that foretold a speedy but not very safe journey home.

She had managed to make her own drink last for the rest of the evening, although she could not imagine why she had let Nick's brief visit deter her. Although she still felt a bit light-headed she was still aware enough to know that driving as he was was not a very wise thing for Donald to do for either of their sakes, but she could not think of an alternative.

'We'll take the long way round,' he informed her as they got into the car. 'I feel like spreading my wings tonight.' He put his arm round her shoulders and pulled her close in a bear hug, his mouth brushing her neck as he buried his face in her hair. 'It's the effect of you, my darling April, you go to my head.'

'Something has,' April remarked wryly, 'but I don't think it's me, Donald.'

He looked down at her, his nice grey eyes glistening

with an expression that was far more typical of Nick. 'Are you insinuating that I've had too much to drink?' he asked solemnly, and April nodded.

'I don't think you ought to drive,' she told him.

'And how,' he asked slowly, 'do you propose to get us home, my darling? You can't drive, can you?'

She shook her head. 'No, I can't,' she agreed. 'But please, Donald—'

'I'll be careful,' he assured her, starting the engine. 'I can drive with my eyes shut, don't you worry.'

She sat, small and quiet, as he took the powerful car out on to the road and changed gear, bringing the speed up as he took the first corner much too fast and brought April's heart into her mouth. She hung on grimly to the side of the car and knew she was shaking nervously as he went faster still, uncaring that the full moon that beamed down on them cast deceptive shadows across the road and flicked sudden dark patches into the car when they passed a higher section of hedge.

Any light-headedness was soon banished by a genuine cold fear as the shadowy hedges flashed past and the narrow, twisting road unfolded with terrifying speed in front of them. The headlights glared brilliantly on tall hazel trees for a moment, then a twist of the wheel sent them flicking into darkness while the road took yet another turn.

They must have been getting close to home, April thought, when the wheel was not turned quite quickly enough and the road did not straighten out as it had done so far but veered crazily off to their right while a grassy ditch yawned at them out of the darkness and, the next moment, swallowed them.

There was surprisingly little noise and the thickness of the hedge took the worst of the collision, but April sat for a moment with her head covered by her arms, not daring to look up. No one moved beside her and she felt a sudden ghastly coldness shiver through her as she looked at Donald.

He too lay with his hands over his head and his fair hair flopped over his forehead, far too quiet for comfort, and April put out a tentative hand to touch his arm. 'Donald!' She thought he moaned slightly and felt relief for that much at least. As best she could she moved him and looked at his face.

It was unmarked and he appeared to be uninjured although unconscious. She felt suddenly completely helpless and looked out at the cold, colourless moonlight that bathed everything around her, making it look alien and frightening. Somewhere along this road she felt sure there was a telephone box. They had not already passed it, she thought, so it must be ahead somewhere, and that was what she must do next – call for help.

She managed to scramble out of the car after some difficulty but not without realizing that she was bruised and stiff, and she stepped out into mud that must have lain there for days, since there had been no rain for almost a week.

She disliked leaving Donald and could not even find a scrap of paper and a pencil to leave a note for him if he should come round while she was gone for help. There was nothing for it but to go, and hope he would be all right there alone.

Before long she began to think that they must have come past the telephone box after all, for there seemed to be no sign of it and she was sure she had walked for miles. Her feet in the thin summer shoes felt tired and ached abominably and her head ached from the after-effects of the vodka. When the elusive kiosk eventually came into view round another corner she was near to tears and ready to cry like a child.

She dialled a number without thinking and was almost surprised when Nick's voice, sharp and faintly distorted by distance, answered. 'April!' He released a breath that she heard quite clearly and gave her no time to speak. 'Where the hell are you?'

'I – I don't exactly know,' she confessed, feeling the first tear roll warningly down her cheeks. 'I'm on the Dardly road somewhere, in – in a telephone box.'

He was silent for a second. 'What happened?' he asked then, more quietly.

'We had an accident in the car and—'

'Are you all right?' He sounded anxious and she hastened to reassure him.

'Yes, I'm all right, but Donald—'

'I don't give a damn what's happened to Donald,' he interrupted again. 'He'd already had too much to drink when I saw him earlier and I don't suppose he had the sense to stop after I left.'

'Oh, Nick, please don't be so – so condemning!' She knew she sounded like a frightened child and, at this moment, she felt like one as she stood there in the small pool of yellow light in the kiosk, clutching her only link with the rest of the world. 'I – I need help and—'

'On the Dardly road,' he said. 'I think I know where you mean. Hang on and I'll be there in about fifteen minutes.'

'I must go back and—'

'You'll stay right where you are,' Nick told her shortly. 'Stay where I can find you, do you hear me?'

'Yes. Yes, Nick.'

He banged the receiver down hard and she could imagine that dark, disapproving frown drawing his brows together as he went out to get his car. No doubt he would think this was yet another of her inevitable mishaps. Perhaps he was of the opinion that two in one day was carrying things too far and he would refuse to help her ever again. It was a dismaying thought and she sat with it miserably on the floor of the telephone box because her knees felt too weak to stand any longer.

Headlights coming along the road a while later brought her to her feet and she breathed a sigh of relief when she saw it was Nick. As she expected he was frowning, but when he saw her dejected expression and the traces of tears still on her cheeks he hugged her briefly and took her back towards the car.

He said nothing, and April felt more miserable than ever, guessing how annoyed he must be at being brought out so late at night. He saw her into the car and went round to his own side, so straight-faced that she wondered if she even dared mention Donald.

'Donald,' she ventured at last, as he slammed the door, 'you — we will go and see if he's all right, won't we?'

He turned and looked at her, looking even more inscrutable than usual in the dim, interior light of the car. 'Of course,' he told her shortly.

'Thank you.'

Silence followed for several minutes as he started the car and drove off back the way she had come, what seemed like hours before. 'Just how far back is he?' he asked.

'I — I don't know,' April confessed. 'I seemed to walk for miles, but it probably wasn't very far, in fact.'

He made no comment, but drove along the narrow lane at a far safer speed than Donald had. 'There he is!' he said suddenly.

The crazily tilted bulk of Donald's car came into view with its headlights still glaring brilliantly amid the dusty leaves of the hedge and its driver still behind the wheel, his head tipped back on the seat as she had left him, as if he was asleep. April felt an awful cold fear in her suddenly at having left him, although there had been little she could have done, but somehow Donald looked so helpless like that and he was still unconscious.

Nick got out, and, after ordering her briefly to stay where she was, went over and stood for a moment beside the other car. He opened the door only with difficulty because of the angle of tilt, then he leaned in and she saw him examining Donald carefully, taking quite some time over it. Apparently satisfied that there was little or no damage done to him, he hauled him out on to the grass verge and April thought she detected the sound of a faint moan.

'Nick!' She stayed where she was, but was unable to resist the urge to call out to him. 'Can I help?'

'You can stay exactly where you are,' Nick replied shortly. 'You've done enough for one evening; I don't want another of your famous accidents to cope with as well. I can manage, thanks.'

April subsided, biting her lip, while he lifted Donald in a fireman's lift and carried him back to the car, putting him in the back seat. Donald opened his eyes briefly as he was put down, and said something under his breath.

'Is – is he all right?' April asked anxiously, drawing comfort from the fact that he had at least made some sound.

'He's perfectly O.K.,' Nick assured her, glancing back at their passenger as he took his own seat. 'If the language he greeted me with over there is anything to go by, I should say he's very much all right.'

'But he's still unconscious, Nick.'

'He's certainly out like a light,' Nick agreed, as he started the engine. 'That's not strictly the same thing. There isn't even a bruise on him, not that shows anyway. He's damned lucky and so are you.'

'But how can you be so sure he's all right?' April insisted, and Nick frowned.

'Take my word for it,' he told her. 'Nothing's broken and he must have cushioned his head on something when you hit that hedge.' He looked at her briefly and curiously. 'Had you moved him?'

'I lifted his head,' April agreed. 'He was leaning on the steering wheel with his head on his arms and I wanted to see if he was all right.'

'Fine way to drive a car round a bend,' Nick remarked acidly. 'But he's had the devil's own luck not being hurt.'

'Maybe – maybe he's worse than you think,' April suggested, worried by Donald's stertorous breathing in the back seat. 'You can't possibly be sure, Nick.'

'I'm not a doctor,' Nick agreed, 'but I'm pretty sure he's in not too bad shape, and I'm *quite* sure that if he's found within a mile of his own car in this state he'll be on a drunken driving charge as sure as eggs. Is that what you want?'

She shook her head. 'No, of course I don't.'

'Then the best thing we can do for him is to get him home, put him to bed, and I'll ring for a garage to come and rescue the car in the morning. That'll give him time to sober up before he has to explain how it got there.'

April looked at him curiously in the dim, ever-changing light that flicked through the windows. The shadows chasing across his face gave him a curiously unreal look, and those strange, tip-tilted eyes looked straight ahead, dark and unfathomable in the semi-darkness.

'Thank you, Nick.' She did not know quite why she had said it like that, answering on Donald's behalf, and it did come into her mind that perhaps Donald would be less grateful for the consideration.

Nick spared her a brief glance over one shoulder, but she was unsure if she saw a small half-smile round his mouth, or if it was a trick of the light. 'What did you expect me to do?' he asked.

'I don't know. I – I suppose I thought you were too angry with him to want to help.' She looked up at the now averted and inscrutable face. 'You sounded angry,' she said, as if her reasoning needed explanation.

'Don't you think I have reason to be?'

'Yes. Yes, of course you have,' she agreed, willingly enough. 'It's very late and – well, perhaps I should have rung someone else.'

He laughed shortly. 'Who, for instance?'

'A – a breakdown van, or – or somebody. I don't know exactly.'

He was silent for a minute. 'What made you ring me?' he asked then, and she frowned curiously, not quite sure herself.

'I don't really know,' she confessed at last. 'I – I just dialled that number without thinking.'

He was definitely smiling now. 'I see.' She wondered if he was as pleased as he sounded. It was never very easy to understand Nick at the best of times, and at this hour, after too much drink and a car accident, she made no attempt to do so.

'I *am* sorry I got you out at this time of night, Nick, honestly,' she told him, and once again he turned his head briefly and smiled at her. 'Had – had you gone to bed?'

'No.'

'I – I thought you were very quick answering the phone,' she said.

'I was waiting for something of the sort to happen,' he said, and April stared at him.

'What do you mean?'

'It was obvious,' he told her, 'that something was bound to happen. Both of you had had too much to drink when I saw you at the club, and Don looked as if he was out to make an evening of it. I would have said something to you then but, the mood you were in, you wouldn't even have given me a hearing, much less believed me, so I just sat tight and hoped for the best. There was nothing else I could do except wait.'

April felt the sudden and inexplicable hammering of her heart and the way the pulse was racing in her temple. 'You – you were waiting up for me?' she asked, and it was a minute or two before he replied.

'I was waiting for something to happen,' he said at last. 'It's no use going to bed when you have the feeling something is going to happen, so I just waited and prayed you wouldn't end your young life in a ditch somewhere.'

He sounded almost facetious about it, but somehow she knew he wasn't, and almost instinctively she reached out a hand and touched his sleeve. 'I'm sorry, Nick.'

'If he had done that to you,' he went on, as if she had not spoken, 'I'd have personally broken Don Jordan into little pieces if he hadn't already done it himself.'

There was nothing, April felt, that she could say in answer to that, so she merely sat quite still beside him as he drove along the moonlit road to Jordan's, while Donald lolled obliviously in the back seat.

Jordan's was in darkness when they arrived, except for one small light over the front door, and April watched, feeling rather helpless as Nick found Donald's key and let them in. He told her to stay in the car while he took Donald up to bed and it was only a very short time before he rejoined her.

Alone in the dimly lit car she had sat and thought about the rather disastrous evening. How one thing had followed on another! First, she decided, she wished Donald had not told her about Fenella and Nick getting married. Not that it mattered to her, of course, except that it would make his sometimes flirtatious manner towards herself very much more discomfiting.

The fact that she had had too many drinks was entirely her own fault and she could not imagine what had prompted her to behave so rashly. Then she should have had the common sense to have insisted on Donald getting a taxi to take them home, no matter how he objected. Getting Nick out in the middle of the night was giving him just one more thing to hold against her and to tease her with. Altogether she wished she had never agreed to come out with Donald but had stayed home and read a book or something else equally safe and uneventful.

By the time Nick came out to drive them home to Kinley she was feeling very much like crying, realizing that it was probably no more than the after-effects of the drinks and the crash. Delayed shock or something of that sort, but still annoyingly weakening when she had to deal with Nick and his inevitable mockery when he discovered her tearful.

They drove back down the narrow lanes in silence and she wondered what he was thinking. If he was feeling annoyed with her or if he was blaming Don for most of it. He garaged the car and they walked to the house together, April blinking in the light from the hall. Her head ached abominably and already there were signs of tears in her eyes again as he turned and closed the door behind them.

'Goodnight, Nick.'

She had hoped to escape upstairs before he noticed that she was crying, but her hope was in vain. He put a detaining hand on her arm as she mounted the first step, and she was more or less obliged to look at him.

'This way,' he said quietly, and took her arm before she could protest, leading her across to the sitting-room. He sat her down in one of the armchairs and walked over to the cabinet in one corner where he poured a generous measure of whisky into a glass. 'Drink this,' he told her, holding out the whisky.

'Nick, you know I don't—'

'I know you've already had enough for one night,' he interrupted, 'but you need something to take the shock out of you.' A gentle finger traced the outline of a faint bruise on her right arm. 'Have you any more of these?' he asked.

'I – I don't know.' She was bound to cry now that he had been so gentle and quiet, and she would almost rather that he had laughed at her as she had expected.

'You don't know,' he mocked her gently, and sat down in another chair, close to her and facing her so that she could not avoid that steady, quizzical gaze.

She clutched the glass of whisky in both hands, feeling them tremble, and the first tears rolled down her face unchecked. 'I – I'd rather go to bed, Nick. Please.'

'Drink that first,' he insisted.

'No, I don't—'

'Drink it, April.'

She pushed the tumbler at him, trying desperately to stop herself from crying. 'I don't want it, please, Nick, don't – don't bully me! Please don't!'

He was beside her in a second and she realized with dismay that she had precipitated the very scene she had sought to avoid. His arms closed round her and she could do nothing but bury her head against his chest and let the tears flow freely. 'I'm not bullying you,' he told her softly, against her ear. 'I'm not, April. I'm just trying to help you, but you won't trust me, will you? You simply won't trust me, and I wish to heaven I knew why.'

She knew she should not have been there in his arms. Not in Nick's arms. It was Donald who loved her, and had told her that Nick was going to marry Fenella Graves. It was quite wrong to be here like this, and even more wrong to feel so little conscience about it. She let herself cry for a few minutes longer while Nick smoothed her hair with one hand, his face resting on the top of her head, his arms so reassuringly strong she felt she would have liked to stay there for ever.

'I – I must go,' she murmured a few minutes later and raised her head, not looking at his eyes but at the firm straightness of his mouth as it crooked upwards in a smile.

'Go where?' he asked softly.

She put her hands to his chest and pushed as hard as she was able, getting up from the chair while he was still momentarily off balance and walking to the door before he could stay her again. 'Goodnight, Nick.' She turned in the doorway and met his eyes, curious and perhaps even faintly amused. 'I – I hope you'll be very happy,' she added, sounding horribly breathless but determined to carry it through. 'You and Fenella.'

'April!'

She heard his cry as she closed the door firmly and quietly behind her, and wondered what he would have said if she had gone back and listened, only, as he had said, she didn't trust him. Neither, she recognized as she ran up the stairs to her room, did she trust herself where Nick was concerned.

CHAPTER ELEVEN

APRIL was not really surprised to find Nick was already gone when she came down to breakfast the following morning, in fact she had planned it that way deliberately. After last night she felt disinclined to face him too early in the morning. His customary light-hearted mockery aimed at her behaviour last night would have been unbearable and she could not have guaranteed that she would not do something rather violent in retaliation.

Equally, she supposed, he had reason to be angry with her about her parting words, for she realized now that she had been horribly indiscreet in betraying the fact that she knew he and Fenella were to marry. That Donald had regretted telling her was obvious, and she should certainly never have spoken to Nick about it in the circumstances. Probably, she thought ruefully, the circumstances were what had prompted her indiscretion, but the damage was done now and all she could do was to try and avoid Nick for as long as possible and hope that by the time she saw him again he would have had time to recover his humour.

Many times during a wakeful night, she had remembered the way he had called after her as she left the room, and she had puzzled over and over what it was he had wanted to say to her. She wished now that she had gone back, but last night she had been much too tired and confused to want to hear anything. Anyway, she told herself, it did not really interest her at all. Donald was the one she was interested in, not Nick, and it was Donald she should be thinking about.

He had already declared himself in love with her and

surely it would not be too long before he took the next step and asked her to marry him. That was something that needed a great deal of consideration, partly because she was not at all sure that she knew him well enough to commit herself either way with certainty.

She sat even longer than usual over her breakfast and even let her coffee get cold while she mused on the possible proposal from Donald and what answer she should give. True, she was very fond of him, but she knew very little about him except as a rather romantic memory from her last visit. He never seemed quite real somehow, and she had never yet decided whether she liked him merely because he was an old admirer or because she found his grown image attractive.

Leaving the dining-room at last, she sighed as she made her way across the hall to see if there was any mail for her. There seldom was, but sometimes Aunt Betty wrote and she always looked, in case. There was only one letter still on the table and that was addressed to her, although it had been forwarded to her from her flat in London.

The writing was somehow familiar, but she could not identify the writer until she saw the signature at the bottom of the single page, and then she smiled to herself. It was from a man with whom she had worked before coming to Kinley and he told her that he had himself left the company they had both worked for and was with someone else. There was a vacancy due soon on the artistic staff and he thought that if she applied for it in good time she stood an excellent chance of getting it. He would, he assured her, recommend her quite willingly.

The information made her smile because she was able to read between the lines. The sender had been one of her most persistent admirers and had always refused to recognize her lack of interest in him. The opportunity of a job however, at a much better salary than she had been getting, was a temptation, no matter who suggested it, and she tapped her lips thoughtfully for a moment with the envelope.

The question of Donald was, momentarily, forgotten as she pondered the new question. She was incredibly reluctant to leave Kinley again, although she knew it was inevitable when her great-uncle considered she had been there long enough. Even more reluctant than she had been seven years before, and she was prepared to admit it.

She thought her great-uncle would probably miss her as much as she would him, and she would miss being with the horses too. Those long, quiet rides in the countryside would be no more than a memory once she got back to town. If she had been prepared to face the fact, she would have admitted, too, to a reluctance to say goodbye to Nick again, but she determinedly avoided that at the moment.

She found her great-uncle in the sitting-room and he looked at her in some surprise when she came in, his shrewd blue eyes searching her face for some explanation as she came nearer.

'Why aren't you out with the horses this morning?' he asked, with typical bluntness, and April smiled.

Seven years ago, even weeks ago, she would have been struck dumb by his manner and the brusqueness of his voice, but now she knew that it was no more than a front for a quite kindly heart and a generous nature, and she took little notice of it.

'I'm going in a few minutes, Uncle Simon,' she told him. 'I just came in to see how you were this morning.'

'Well enough,' the old man informed her shortly. 'Though it's no thanks to folks clumping about half the night.'

April pulled a rueful face. 'I'm sorry if we woke you,'

she said, 'but we – I mean I was rather late coming in, I'm afraid.'

'I thought you were out with young Jordan. *Were* you?' It was more statement than question, and it sounded very much like an accusation, but April tried to ignore the small niggle of resentment she felt, and nodded. Evidently he had not seen Nick this morning either and was still in ignorance of the events of last night which left her wishing that she had not come in to see him, then Nick would have been left to do the explaining.

'I went out with Donald, Uncle Simon. We went to a little pub he knew and then on to a country club.'

'Hmm.' He obviously did not approve of that very much, but he refrained from saying so at the moment. 'You came in with Nick, didn't you?'

His weak eyes studied her narrowly and she wondered just how much she should tell him. 'Yes. Yes, I came back with Nick,' she agreed.

'And I heard him come back a good hour before,' he snapped, the weak eyes regarding her suspiciously, as if he suspected her of trying to deceive him.

April flushed, the resentment beginning to rear its head. 'You probably did,' she told him. 'I rang him about half past twelve.'

'Heard the phone,' the old man told her. 'Noisy damned thing at that hour of the night.' She would have apologized for rousing him so late, but he gave her no time and she began to feel like a prisoner undergoing interrogation. In a lot of ways Nick was incredibly like him. 'What happened? Did you have to get Nick to rescue you from Don Jordan?'

'Of course not!' She looked at him indignantly. 'I – we had an accident in Donald's car, and I was the only one able to go for help.'

'So you rang Nick?'

'Yes,' she admitted. 'I can't think why, but I was a bit fuddled myself.'

'Best thing you could have done,' he told her, gruffly approving. 'Is young Jordan badly hurt?'

April shook her head. 'No, thank goodness. Nick said he was O.K. anyway, and he seemed to know. We took him home and Nick put him to bed.'

The shrewd old eyes quizzed her closely. 'Why couldn't he put himself to bed?' he demanded, and April avoided looking at him while she sought an answer.

'He – he wasn't really very well,' she said.

The old man studied her face for a moment, then snorted his disgust at the obvious untruth. 'Damn it! Was he drunk, April?'

'He – he had had a few drinks,' she admitted, cautiously, because he looked so angry. 'But then so had I.'

He chose to ignore her part in it, but seemed bent on making the most of Donald's misdemeanour. 'And he had no more sense than to drive you home?' he demanded. 'I wonder Nick didn't teach him a lesson,' he added. 'He might have killed you in that great noisy car he drives. Damn it, Nick should have thrashed him, not coddled him to his bed.'

His violence startled her and she wondered what he would have to say to Nick about it when he saw him. 'Nick wouldn't do such a thing,' she objected. 'Donald was unconscious and there was nothing else to do but put him to bed. We left his car in the ditch, but Nick said he'd be in bad trouble for driving while he was – well, a bit the worse for drink, so he got him away so that he could sober up before he had to account for the car being in the ditch.'

'Soft!' The old man snorted derisively. 'Soft as butter, young Nick. I suppose he was doing it to please you.'

The suggestion startled her and she looked it. 'I shouldn't think so for one minute,' she denied. 'He likes Donald and he didn't want to see him get into too much trouble.'

'Rubbish!' he retorted. 'He's not that friendly with Don Jordan that he'd take a risk like that for him. And don't look so innocent, my girl, you know quite well Nick would do anything to please you. If you don't you're a bigger fool than I took you for.'

She could feel the colour warm her cheeks and bit on her lip, anger and embarrassment fighting for precedence. 'I'm not a fool, Uncle Simon,' she told him. 'You're quite wrong about Nick. He – he has his own plans, and pleasing me doesn't come into it.'

She told herself, a moment later, that she should have been less rash in seeking a reason for her denial, but having dangled the carrot she knew the old man would not rest until he knew the rest of it, unless she had misjudged him. It was inevitable that he would not take at all kindly to Nick marrying Fenella Graves, but it was not really her place to tell tales on Nick and he could be forgiven in this instance for being angry with her.

'I think you'd better explain that, my girl,' he told her in a tone that left no room for argument.

'Oh – there's really nothing to explain.' She sought to remedy, at least in part, some of the harm she may have done. 'It's – it's just that Nick doesn't care whether he pleases me or not. Why should he?'

He looked at her for a moment in silence and she found the experience unnerving. 'You *are* a fool,' he said at last, with devastating bluntness.

April did not look at him but ran one finger along a dust-free edge of a table, her expression determinedly blank. 'Maybe I am,' she agreed quietly. 'Now I think I'd better go and exercise the horses, before I'm accused of slacking.' She remembered her letter as she turned to go and held it in her hand as she turned again. 'I have the opportunity of getting a good job in London,' she told him. 'Much better pay than I was getting before and George, the man who wrote and told me about it, thinks I stand a very good chance of getting it.'

'He's a beau of yours?' The question was blunt and she found the old-fashioned term beau very unsuitable when applied to a very modern George, but she didn't smile as she felt inclined to do.

'In a way, I suppose you could say so,' she admitted. 'Although I never encouraged him.'

He looked at her narrow-eyed, as if he only half believed her. 'You're not going?'

'I might,' she told him. 'It's too good to turn down, Uncle Simon, and I may not have another chance like this.'

'Does Nick know?'

The question was unexpected and, for a moment, she looked at him uncertainly. 'No,' she said at last. 'I've only just had the letter and I haven't seen Nick this morning yet.' She pushed the letter back into her pocket again, and pondered for several moments before she spoke. 'I'm going to ride over and see how Donald is this morning,' she told him, 'and see what he thinks about it.'

'Does it concern him?' She thought he resented having Donald consulted, but she nodded, a small frown drawing at her brows.

'I think it will,' she said. 'He – I think he wants to marry me.'

The old man's grey head came up sharply and his eyes narrowed. 'Oh, he does, does he?'

April knew he was going to argue and she steeled herself not to lose her temper. 'He's implied as much,' she informed him. 'He – he says he loves me.'

'Tcch!' A scornful hand dismissed such things as unimportant. 'He was always moon-eyed over you when you were here before. He's just never grown up.'

April flushed, her eyes sparkling blue as she defied him on that particular subject, because she felt she knew far more about it than he did. 'I happen to believe him,' she told him. 'And I also believe loving someone is important.' She was growing rash with anger and forgot about her determination not to lose her temper. 'Besides, I don't see why you should find my marrying Donald any more undesirable than Nick marrying Fenella Graves.'

Now, she thought a breathless second later, she had really done it. Her great-uncle seemed almost to have stopped breathing for a full minute and his eyes had a cold, hard glitter that made her shiver.

'So,' he said slowly, at last, '*that's* what his game is, is it?'

'Oh no! I mean – oh, I don't know for certain, Uncle Simon, honestly. Only what Donald told me.'

The sharp eyes held her unwilling gaze until she could stand it no longer and turned away. 'And where did *he* get it from?' the old man demanded.

'From – from Fenella.'

He was silent for so long that she turned back to him, both anxious and curious, but he was merely sitting there like some ancient god of vengeance, nodding his head and with a small, rather malicious smile on his face. 'We'll see about that,' he said ominously quiet. 'We'll see whether Miss Fenella Graves is as keen to marry him when she knows he isn't going to get anything in my will.'

'Oh no!' April was appalled at what she had done, and she trembled to think what Nick would have to say to her. Standing there with her hands to her face she desperately sought some solution that would undo all the harm she had done. 'Oh, Uncle Simon, please, please don't do that.

Please don't blame Nick.'

'Who else do I blame?' he asked shortly. 'You shouldn't be pleading his case, my girl, you'll be the better off if he doesn't get anything.'

She shook her head blindly. 'I – I don't want it. Not if it means taking it from Nick – I don't want any of it.'

'You're a fool, girl.'

'Maybe I am,' April said, her voice half-choked in her throat when she thought of becoming twice as rich because she had betrayed a confidence before Nick could tell his stepfather what his plans were. It was hideously unfair and she wished she had never come to Kinley again, or that Donald had never told her about Fenella Graves marrying Nick. She looked down at the old man, puzzled by some air of secrecy about him that she could not rightly interpret. 'I – I'd rather not have anything at all, Uncle Simon, than have Nick think I told you deliberately so that you'd cut him out of your will.'

'If he marries the Graves girl he'll not get a penny of my money,' the old man vowed coldly. 'I'll not let her get her hands on it.'

'But—'

'He knows I don't like her,' he went on, unheeding. 'He knows what I think of her. She's a fortune-hunter, just like her mother was – after everything she can get.'

'But she has money of her own,' April protested, desperately trying to repair the damage she had done, even if it meant defending Fenella Graves. 'And she loves Nick.'

Old Simon eyed her narrowly. 'How do you know that?'

The question confounded her for a moment, then she shook her head slowly, her hands clasped together as if in prayer. 'She – she does,' she insisted. 'Of course she does,

Uncle Simon. She must do.'

'Must she?' He reached out and she came and stood beside him, while he took her two hands, his voice sounding unexpectedly gentle suddenly as he looked up at her. 'Why must she?'

'Because—' April kept her eyes lowered. 'Because he's Nick, and – and Donald says he's – well, that he's very popular with women.'

'Don Jordan talks too much,' the old man opined sharply, but he was actually smiling.

'Uncle Simon!' She felt she must take advantage of his better mood to speak up again for Nick. 'You – you won't cut Nick out of your will, will you?'

There was neither encouragement nor repulsion in his expression and she did not quite know what to think. 'If he marries Fenella Graves,' he told her, less vehemently than before. 'I will – and he knows it.'

'Uncle Simon—'

He patted her hand with that strange unexpected gentleness and shook his head. 'You go and help with the horses,' he told her. 'I'll sort out young Nick when the need arises.'

It was a surprise in a way to find Donald up and around when she arrived at the farm, but April was enormously relieved to see him. Not least because she had not been one hundred per cent sure that Nick's diagnosis was correct.

He looked up and smiled, a little sheepishly, when she rode into the yard, and came across at once to help her down. 'Are you still speaking to me?' he asked, and tentatively kissed her forehead as he set her on her feet.

'Of course I am, why shouldn't I?' She smiled up at him, noting the dark shadows under his eyes and the slight paleness that showed beneath his tan. 'How are you this morning?'

He pulled a wry face. 'I feel as if I've been run over by a steamroller,' he said, 'and by all accounts I was lucky to get off as lightly as I did.' He looked most appealingly contrite and she found herself reaching for his hand in consolation. 'I don't quite know how to say how I feel about involving you in what could have been a very bad accident, April. I've never got drunk before and driven afterwards and I hadn't really an excuse for it. I don't know why I did it, but I'm very sorry and I promise it will never happen again.'

It was quite a touching little speech, and she squeezed his hand to let him know she understood and bore no malice. 'I know it won't happen again,' she said. 'And, as you can see, I'm not hurt. You have a rather nasty hang-over this morning, but otherwise neither of us is any the worse for the incident, so I suggest we just put it down to experience and say no more about it.'

He looked down at her for a moment without speaking, then shook his head. 'You're far more lenient than I have any right to expect,' he told her, at last, 'and much more lenient than Nick was.'

'Nick?' She looked at him curiously. 'He said he was going to ring the garage this morning and get them to collect your car. Did he tell you?'

Donald nodded, his expression rueful. 'He did,' he said. 'He also read me the riot act while I was still trying to get my head to stay on my shoulders this morning. I fully expected him to hit me, but he evidently thought better of it at the last moment.'

April stared at him. 'You mean he's been over here this morning?'

'He certainly has.' He led the way into the house, a rather thoughtful frown between his brows. 'That's how I know what an idiot I made of myself last night. He left no phrase unturned to let me know exactly what he thought of me.'

'I'm sorry, Donald.' She was unsure just what her reaction was to the news. It was certainly unexpected to find that Nick had still been angry enough this morning to be so abusive to Donald, but she wished she knew more about his reason. It was unlike Nick to lose his temper at all and even less like him to carry it on so long, unless he felt that family feelings had been offended. He had a very strong feeling for his stepfather's family, just as the old man had.

Donald looked a bit surprised at her showing sympathy, but gratified, nevertheless. 'I suppose I asked for it,' he allowed, 'but Nick has a tongue like a whiplash when he feels strongly enough about anything and he really let fly this morning.' He looked at her curiously. 'I gather you fetched him out last night.'

She nodded, still puzzling over Nick's unusual behaviour. 'Yes, I did. Though heaven knows why, and I'd never have done it if I'd thought he was going to make such a fuss about it.'

Donald shrugged, seemingly prepared to let Nick get away with his outburst as long as April was in sympathy with him. 'It could have been very much worse, April. You could have been injured or even killed if we hadn't been incredibly lucky, so I suppose he has cause to be angry. He's threatened me with instant death if I risk your neck again,' he added, 'and frankly I believe him.'

April could not resist a smile at that. 'Oh, Nick's bark is worse than his bite in most instances,' she said, surprised to find herself believing it. 'He was anxious enough to make sure you weren't found with your car last night. He said it would give you time to sober up before anyone started asking questions.'

'Very thoughtful of him,' Donald declared, with a hint

of sarcasm. 'But I rather think he was only concerned about that because you were with me.'

'Family honour again?' she asked, and he held her gaze for a moment steadily before lowering his eyes.

'Perhaps,' he said, leaving April with a curious feeling in her stomach that fluttered nervously and set her mind darting in every direction at once.

They went into the small cosy sitting-room and he saw her into a chair, then walked over to the window where he stood with his back to her. He had his hands in his pockets and there was a curious kind of tenseness about the set of his shoulders and the way he held his head. It was a moment or two before he spoke and April waited, wondering what was on his mind that required such concentrated thought.

When he at last broke the silence, he spoke without turning round and she wondered if she imagined the rather despondent air about him. 'I – I suppose I've no hope of getting anywhere with you now, have I, April?'

She looked at him for a moment, wondering how best to answer. If it had been meant as merely a plea for forgiveness for last night's accident, it would have been fairly easy to tell him he need not worry, but she felt he was referring to something more serious than that and she hesitated.

'Getting anywhere?' She felt rather cowardly for merely repeating his words, but she had to think.

'I mean,' he told her, 'I don't suppose you'd even consider mârrying me now that you know how – how erratic and unreliable I can be.'

It was obvious that much depended on her answer and she felt she must think carefully before she spoke. She had half expected him to propose to her soon, but to ask her now and in such circumstances, she felt, was rather unfair, and she was horribly unsure of both herself and of her feelings for him.

As if he had already guessed her answer he turned round from the window and from the way he looked at her she knew he was going to take any refusal rather badly. 'You don't have to say it, April,' he told her slowly. 'And I can't really blame you after last night.'

He turned back to the window again and April got to her feet, walking over to stand just behind him. 'Oh, Donald, please don't say that! I've already told you that I don't hold any malice for last night, I'm prepared to forget about it if you are.'

He half-turned his head and looked down at her over one shoulder, his nice grey eyes so unhappy she felt she could have wept. 'I'm glad about that anyway,' he told her. 'But the answer is still no, isn't it, April?'

She put a hand round his arm and hesitated for a moment before answering. 'I – I'd rather say it was perhaps, Donald,' she told him, and raised a finger to his lips when he would have spoken. 'I'm not at all sure how I feel about anything at the moment, and I'd like time to think about anything as important as marriage.'

'Of course you would.' He put a hand over hers, clasped round his arm, and his eyes had a more hopeful look in them now. 'You're not leaving Kinley yet, are you? There's plenty of time to think about it.'

She sighed, remembering another decision she had to make. 'I don't know, Donald. I've heard of a very good job in London and I'm not sure I can afford not to apply for it at least.'

'But you won't leave yet?' He looked as if he feared he would never see her again once she left Kinley.

'I don't know when it would be, always providing I got the job, of course,' she told him. 'But I think I should try for it.'

His reply was so incredibly like her great-uncle's that

she stared at him for a moment before she answered. 'Does Nick know about it?' he asked.

April shook her head, and frowned. 'No, he doesn't,' she said. 'And what's more I don't see why everyone should expect me to tell him. It's none of his concern, and I'm sure he couldn't care less whether I come or go. He has other fish to fry.'

'You mean Fenella?' He looked uneasy. 'I'm not sure I should have told you about that, April. I hope you won't mention it to anyone else.'

April looked down at her hands, unwilling to admit that it was already too late. 'I'm – I'm afraid I already have,' she confessed. 'I told Uncle Simon.'

'Oh, lord!' His look of dismay was almost comical.

'He's furious about it,' April told him, 'and I dread to think what he'll say to Nick. I shouldn't have said anything, Donald, I'm sorry.'

He shook his head. 'It's Nick I'm thinking of,' he said. 'I've already had a sample of his temper and I don't relish being the cause of another outburst like this morning.'

'I know.' She gloomily considered her own future. 'It might be just as well if I did leave,' she said. 'I'm going to be very unpopular at Kinley.'

'Oh, but they wouldn't do that,' he protested. 'Expect you to leave, I mean. Surely not.'

April pulled a rueful face, less optimistic than he was. 'In the circumstances I might prefer to go. It could be quite unbearable for a while.'

'But—' He sought for reasons why she should stay. 'You'll hate it back in London, April. You love it here, don't you?' She nodded. 'And then there's Starlight – you won't like leaving the foal behind you, will you? And you can't very well take him with you.'

April looked at him, shocked by her own forgetfulness. 'Starlight!' she said. 'Oh, how could I have forgotten him like that?'

'You couldn't leave him,' Donald told her, pressing home his advantage. 'So you can't go, can you?'

'I can't stay much longer in any case,' April said. 'Uncle Simon asked me to stay for two or three months and I've been here about two months now.'

'Oh, but I'm sure he didn't mean it literally,' Donald insisted. 'You get on well with the old man now, don't you? Now that you're older.'

'I get on very well with him,' April agreed. 'Or at least I did until now. Now I'm not so sure. I'm rather fond of him, actually, although he's not always an easy man to understand.'

'Then he won't want you to leave.'

'Maybe not.' She could not tell Donald how much her uncle disliked Fenella and his threat to disown Nick if he married her. Only she knew how unbearable it would be if Nick chose to blame her for his stepfather's change of mind about leaving him half his fortune.

'Of course he won't want you to go,' Donald was insisting. 'He likes having you there.'

'As long as I'm earning my keep,' April said wryly. 'He doesn't like the idea of anyone being a lady of leisure, not when they're young and healthy, so I shall have to find another job soon.'

'But you don't sit around doing nothing,' he said, seeking every means to persuade her. 'You help Nick in the stable.'

April reluctantly faced another fact that she had not, until now, realized – her helping Nick with the stable. She smiled wryly. 'I don't imagine,' she told him, 'that I shall be allowed to work with Nick for very much longer. Not if he's marrying Fenella.'

'No. Perhaps not,' he allowed. 'I suppose Fenella wouldn't like it, would she? Any more than I do.'

'Fenella hates it,' April assured him, 'much more than you do.'

Riding back across the meadow some time later, April was relieved to have been able to get away from the farm without having committed herself to a firm answer. She had agreed to stay on at Kinley as long as her great-uncle made her welcome and Donald had seemed satisfied with that. While she was there, he said, there was hope for him.

Now that she was on her own again April's mind turned once more to the problem of Nick and her own indiscretion to her great-uncle. She could not believe that the old man would cut Nick right out of his will and yet, on the other hand, he was a stubborn old man and he disliked Fenella intensely.

She sighed in sympathy with herself and wished she had never been told about it. She had no more liking for Fenella than her great-uncle had, and she was prepared to believe that his stepfather's fortune had something to do with Nick's attraction for Fenella, but also she was convinced that the money was not the only reason.

No one could deny that Nick was a dangerously attractive man, April least of all, and the pity was that he had not chosen another of his numerous conquests to marry instead of the one woman his stepfather hated. She had never doubted for one minute that Donald's information about the number of women Nick knew was true, and Nick himself had not denied it even when she challenged him with it.

She sighed again as she rode Dingo back to the paddock, her mind so preoccupied that she even failed to realize that there was anyone else about until Nick stepped out from the backing hedge and stood facing her in what she could only term a threatening attitude.

His arms were folded across his chest and his dark brows were drawn close together above those strange, unfathomable eyes. The eyes themselves regarded her with less favour, she thought, than she would have imagined possible, and they watched her as she unsaddled Dingo and turned him free without venturing a word.

When she had finished he took the saddle from her as she would have walked past him on her way to the stable, and hung it over the top rail of the fence. She looked at him warily, with her heart beating wildly against her ribs. She did not need to be clairvoyant to know that he had seen Uncle Simon.

'Nick—' She had some vague notion of trying to placate him, but she knew, even before she spoke, that it would be useless.

'Shut up!' he told her shortly. 'For once in your life keep quiet and listen.'

'I know what you're angry about,' she said, breathlessly and desperately trying to justify herself. 'And – and I don't blame you, Nick, not in the least. I know I shouldn't have said anything to Uncle Simon, and – and I'm sorry, I really am.'

'You'll be a darned sight sorrier if you don't stop chattering and let me get a word in sideways,' he warned her.

'I'm sorry.'

'So you said. Closing the stable door, as usual.'

'What do you mean?' she asked, genuinely puzzled, and he sighed.

'It means that you always speak first and think about the consequences afterwards when it's too late,' he informed her shortly. 'You just can't resist listening to every lurid tale you hear about me and then repeating them, can you?'

'Oh, Nick, I don't!'

'You do,' he insisted relentlessly. 'You informed me that I was some sort of – of Casanova weeks ago, according to your friend Donald Jordan, that is. Now you take it into your head to tell Pop that I'm marrying Fenella – on the same authority, apparently.'

'Oh, Nick, honestly, I didn't think—'

'You never do,' Nick retorted, 'that's the trouble.'

April had never felt so small, miserable and misjudged, and she held on to the paddock fence with one hand as if she needed its support. 'He was being sarcastic about – about Donald wanting to marry me,' she explained dolefully, 'and I told him I didn't see that it was any worse than you wanting to marry Fenella.'

Surprisingly he looked at her silently for a moment, and she thought he wore a slightly wary expression. 'Has he asked you to marry him?' he asked.

April kept her eyes lowered. 'Well, yes, in a way he has.'

'What's that supposed to mean? In a way?'

'I – I mean in a way he *has* asked me to marry him, and—'

Nick snorted impatiently. 'There's only one way to ask a girl to marry you, that I know of,' he declared shortly. 'That's to ask the question and get a yes or no in answer.'

April flushed to hear it brought down to such basic principles, and she was prepared to argue the point, if need be. 'It's not always as easy as that,' she told him. 'Donald did ask me to marry him, but not straight out like that.'

'But he did ask you?' He seemed far more interested at the moment in discovering just where she stood with Donald than he did about his own position.

April nodded. 'Yes,' she said. 'He asked me.'

'What did you say?'

April looked at him steadily, a little more sure of herself now, than she had been at the outset. 'I don't see that that need concern you,' she told him, forgetting for the moment that it was a rather provocative answer in the circumstances.

She saw the brief, swift flash of anger in his eyes again. 'As much as my affairs concern you,' he rapped. 'And I shan't relay them to all and sundry either.'

'Nick!'

He shook his head after a second's silence, and she thought she could already detect an easing of the tension. 'Why on earth did you have to tell Pop that tale about Fenella?' he asked.

'I told you, he was being sarcastic about—'

'And you just let it drop on the spur of the moment,' he said resignedly. 'Even though you knew he'd be furious about it.' Her nod admitted it. 'Is that why you did it?'

'Oh no, Nick, you know it isn't!'

'It beats me,' he said, shaking his head. 'You might have known he'd be mad enough to cut me out of his will if I ever married Fenella, but you still told him.'

April sought for words. She *should* have known that the first thing Uncle Simon would do would be to cut Nick out of his will, but it had not even occurred to her at the time, and now it was too late. 'I – I couldn't help it,' she said, and he shook his head again, his expression now more resigned than angry.

'I don't know what I'm going to do about you,' he told her slowly. 'You bring me more trouble than any woman I ever knew. You're in and out of one scrape after another and you're an incorrigible gossip.'

'I'm not!' April denied vehemently, biting on her lip. 'I'm *not* a gossip, Nick.'

'You listen to any and every tale Don Jordan likes to

pass on about me,' he went on relentlessly. 'You've turned my whole existence upside down until I feel like getting out and leaving you in sole possession.'

'Oh, Nick, no!'

'But on second thoughts,' he said, 'I don't see why I should be the one who comes off worst.'

It would not be long now, April thought wildly, before she broke down and wept like a baby, and this time it was unlikely that she would be offered that consoling shoulder to cry on. She drew a deep breath and determinedly swallowed the threatening tears. 'All right, Nick,' she said, her voice sounding horribly husky and uncertain. 'I'll go.'

'Where?' He sounded far more amused than worried about it, and she shook her head miserably.

'I – I have a chance of a very good post with a big advertising firm,' she said chokily. 'I – I was leaving anyway.'

'Oh, yes, the letter Pop told me about. From one of your boy-friends, wasn't it?'

'No, it wasn't,' April denied, tearfully indignant. 'I worked with him, that's all.'

'Pop said he was an admirer,' he insisted, and April glared at him through her tears.

'Now *you're* listening to gossip,' she retorted. 'But I suppose it's all right for you, isn't it?'

He said nothing, but laughed softly, and she turned, half-blinded by the tears that now rolled dismally down her cheeks, and ran as fast as her shaking legs would carry her, across the garden and into the house. She did not pause until she reached her own room and there she flung herself down on the bed and sobbed as she had not done since she was a small child.

Nothing, nothing at all, would persuade her to stay on at Kinley now that she knew exactly what Nick thought of her. His words went round and round in her head and she could find no scrap of comfort in any of them.

It was time she went back to London and took another job, became an independent soul again. Uncle Simon would understand, although he had not seemed very encouraging when she mentioned George's letter to him. She had so enjoyed being at Kinley that it had never occurred to her that Nick found her such a trial. Even his teasing had been more mischievous than malicious, that she had never realized how she annoyed him. The sooner she went away the better, she decided. Perhaps even tomorrow, for her flat was still available and she could soon pack her things.

She sat up on the bed at last, and wiped away the remaining tears with a wet handkerchief, pulling a rueful face at her reflection in the dressing-table mirror. Her hair was dishevelled and needed combing, and her eyes were red-rimmed with crying. Even Donald, devoted as he was, would think twice about asking her to marry him, if he could see her now.

It was lunch time before she left her room and she did so with a thousand and one qualms about telling Uncle Simon of her decision to leave. He could not stop her, of course, and the way she felt at the moment, she did not care if he threatened to cut her out of his will too. She could not stay on at Kinley, not now.

Apart from a little puffiness around her eyes she looked quite normal when she went downstairs to lunch, and she determined that she would not cry again, no matter what provocation she was offered. Her departure must be as quiet and dignified as possible.

She had rather hoped, perhaps optimistically, that Nick would not be in for lunch, but he was there when she came in, standing by the window with his stepfather, both of them turning together when she appeared.

The old man's eyes studied her shrewdly, although she realized that from that distance he could barely see her.

Nick's reaction she was uncertain of, for those strange eyes of his could be completely inscrutable when it suited him. 'I – I hope I'm not late,' she ventured, when neither of them spoke.

'You're not late at all,' the old man assured her, with that unexpected gentleness he had shown earlier. 'We're ready whenever you are, April.'

They were more than half way through lunch before she dared even mention her decision to leave, and then she thought the old man looked less surprised than he should have been, and she glanced suspiciously at Nick.

'I don't know why you've made up your mind to go so suddenly,' he told her, 'but you must do as you think fit, of course, my girl.'

'You – you don't mind?' She had secretly hoped that he would try to dissuade her, then at least she would have known that her stay had not been a trial for them both.

'I'd rather you stayed,' the old man told her quietly, 'but I doubt if I'm the one to persuade you to change your mind.'

'It's better if I go, Uncle Simon,' she told him. 'I can apply for this job I've heard about and – and – well, it's best, I think. I'm – I'm sorry if I've been a disappointment to you.'

'You haven't,' he told her, and she smiled gratefully.

Nick had said very little all through lunch and she looked across at him from under her lashes, hastily lowering her eyes again when she met his. 'I've packed my things,' she said, her voice quavering horribly. 'I'd like to stay until tomorrow, if you don't mind.'

The old man nodded, and the rest of the meal was taken in almost complete silence, then her great-uncle got up from the table and stood for a long moment looking down at her. 'Don't be too hasty, April,' he said quietly, and flicked a brief glance at his stepson before going out of the room.

Nick was the last person she wanted to be left alone with at the moment, and April hastily got up and would have walked out of the room in the wake of the old man if Nick too had not risen to his feet and walked round the table to block her way.

'Please, Nick!'

She could not bear it if he asked her to stay on, as she suspected his stepfather had told him to, just because the old man wanted it that way. But there was something in the way he was looking at her that made her heart skip disturbingly and she wondered what more he could possibly have to say to her that would not add to her unhappiness.

'April.'

'No, Nick, please!'

His hands took hers gently as she fought against a new and exciting fear, and he pulled her to him so that she could feel the steady, firm beat of his heart under her fingers. 'Please listen,' he said softly.

'You – you needn't try and persuade me,' she told him huskily, 'just because Uncle Simon told you to.'

'Is that what you think I'm doing?' She chanced a swift glance upwards and saw the old and almost unbearably familiar smile in his eyes.

'You said I'd – I'd turned your whole existence upside down,' she said, recalling the words only too plainly. 'You said I'd brought you more trouble than any woman you've ever known.'

'So you have.'

She tried to free her hands, her eyes reproachful, but he held on to her much too firmly for that. 'Then why do you bother asking me to stay on?' she asked.

'I didn't ask you,' he countered.

'Oh, Nick! You never take anything I say seriously, do you?' she said in despair, and one hand lifted her chin so that she found it difficult not to look at him.

'Only when you carry fairy-tales to Pop about me,' he said softly, and she looked up again to meet the gentle mockery he regarded her with.

'Fairy-tales?'

He nodded. 'I *was* angry about that, and I think I had a right to be. Actually,' he added wryly, 'I suppose I should blame Don Jordan as much as you. You only pass on the gossip, don't you?'

'That's a horrible thing to say,' April protested.

'But true, sweet coz,' he taunted, laughing at her now as he always did.

'Donald says Fenella told him you and she were getting married,' April insisted, 'and I believe him.'

'Then you should have more sense than to believe Fen,' he told her.

April regarded him for a moment with wide, doubtful eyes. 'You – you mean you're *not* going to marry Fenella?' she asked, and he nodded slowly.

'I'm not going to marry Fenella,' he echoed.

'Then she—'

'She was talking through her hat,' he informed her inelegantly.

'But why?'

Nick smiled slowly. 'Oh, come on, darling,' he said softly. 'You accused *me* of being obtuse on that point once, remember?'

'You – you mean she's – jealous?'

He nodded, smiling at her reticence. 'I mean she's jealous,' he agreed.

'But I thought—'

He sighed deeply. 'Darling April, you never *do* think,

that's the whole trouble, otherwise you'd know that I wouldn't marry Fenella in a million years.'

'Oh!'

'Any more than you'd marry Don Jordan.'

'I don't know that I—'

'I do,' Nick interrupted with a laugh. 'I love you and I've no intention of letting Don Jordan beat me to it.'

'Nick!'

'As I told you,' he went on, disregarding her breathless interjection and the way she was shaking her head as she tried to think straight, 'you've turned my whole existence upside down and you've got me into such a state of desperation that I felt like getting out.'

'I thought you were – were fed up with me,' she said, still not quite believing it.

'So I am,' Nick declared, 'but I doubt if I could go back to my quiet, tranquil existence without you, now.'

'Nick—' This time he silenced her in an even more effective way and she had only breath enough to bury her face against his chest when at last he released her.

'You're such a little chatterbox,' he informed her, his voice muffled by her hair. 'But I'm stuck with you and I suppose I can always gag you when you get too much. Unless Pop throws us both out, of course,' he added thoughtfully, and April lifted her face again to look at him, her eyes huge and shining.

'I have a feeling,' she told him, 'that when I marry you, I shall be doing exactly what Uncle Simon wants me to do.'

'*When* you marry me,' Nick echoed, his arms tightening. 'Does that mean you haven't outgrown your schoolgirl crush on me after all?'

April laughed softly, meeting those strange, tip-tilted eyes that could do such odd things to her heartbeat. 'I can't have done,' she told him. 'I still go weak at the knees whenever I look at you, and that must mean I love you, mustn't it?'

'Oh, it must do,' Nick assured her solemnly, and kissed her again to prove it.

Each month from Harlequin

8 NEW FULL LENGTH ROMANCE NOVELS

ALL BOOKS 60c

These titles are available at your local bookseller, or through the Harlequin Reader Service, M.P.O. Box 707, Niagara Falls, N.Y. 14302; Canadian address 649 Ontario St., Stratford, Ont.

FREE!!!

Did you know . . . . . . ?

that just by mailing in the coupon below you can receive a brand new, up-to-date "Harlequin Romance Catalogue" listing literally hundreds of Harlequin Romances you probably thought were out of print.

Now you can shop in your own home for novels by your favorite Harlequin authors — the Essie Summers you wanted to read, the Violet Winspear you missed, the Mary Burchell you thought wasn't available anymore!

They're all listed in the "Harlequin Romance Catalogue". And something else too — the books are listed in numerical sequence, — so you can fill in the missing numbers in your library.

Don't delay — mail the coupon below to us today. We'll promptly send you the "Harlequin Romance Catalogue"

FREE!

Have You Missed Any of These
Harlequin Romances?

All books are 60c. Please use the handy order coupon.

X

Have You Missed Any of These
Harlequin Romances?

All books are 60c. Please use the handy order coupon.

z